PROMISE ME

DARA GIRARD

ISBN 13: 978-1949764291

PROMISE ME

Published by ILORI Press Books

This is a work of fiction. Names, characters, places and incidents are either the product of the author's imagination or are used fictitiously, and any resemblance to actual persons, living or dead, business establishments, events or locales is entirely coincidental.

ILORI PRESS BOOKS, LLC

PO Box #10332

Silver Spring, MD 20914

www.iloripressbooks.com

The Black Stockings Society

Power Play

A Gentleman's Offer

Body Chemistry

Round the Clock

Return of the Black Stockings Society

Playing for Keeps

After Hours

A Private Affair

Just One Look

Private Lessons

Henson Series

Table for Two

Familiar Stranger

Gaining Interest

Careless Rapture

Dangerous Curves

Duvall Sisters

The Glass Slipper Project

Taming Mariella

A Reluctant Hero

The Clifton Sisters

The Sapphire Pendant

The Amber Stone

The Emerald Ring

It Happened One Wedding

Unexpected Pleasure

Midnight Promise

Sweet Temptation

Always and Forever

Truly Yours

Novels

Illusive Flame

Honest Betrayal

The Daughters of Winston Barnett

Remember My Name

CHAPTER ONE

*H*e stopped holding his breath.

He hadn't realized he'd stopped breathing until he felt the tension in his chest ease. He was safe. Everything was perfect.

She'd said yes.

Victory. It was the end of a Disney film. He was Aladdin and she was Jasmine. He was Simba and she was Nala.

Today, this moment, had changed the rest of his life. *He'd convinced Esme Scott to marry him!* Bryant Hill resisted the urge to leap up and shout with joy. He thought his heart would burst from happiness as he slid the engagement ring on her finger. Esme Scott. Beautiful, successful Esme. The daughter of Marlon Scott, the president of Scott Designs, Inc. where he worked as a toy designer.

If he were to sculpt a toy to fit her, he would pay special attention to her brown skin (he'd have to get the shade just right, focusing on the honeyed undertone), her fine high forehead, sharp dark eyes, fine mouth and black hair that fell in waves to her shoulders. Naturally she'd have a superpower—more than one because she was multi-talented—one power would be the ability to make fire appear out of thin air, she'd also be able to fly, mind read and hypnotize. She'd done that to him many times.

He was under her spell and loved every second of it. Gaining her favor had been a hard won victory. Two years of effort. And it had been worth it. She'd said yes.

To him.

Bryant pressed his mouth against her sweet lips, wondering when his heart would stop racing; when he wouldn't feel like his tie was a snake around his neck slowly suffocating him. Perhaps he'd wanted this more than he'd realized. He wanted her more than he'd allowed himself to admit until this moment.

Then why didn't he feel relieved? She'd said yes, why did he still feel as if he could lose her?

Bryant drew away from her and stared down at the engagement ring on her long, slim finger. It wasn't an illusion. It was really there and he hadn't misheard her. She'd said yes. Yes. Yes! They now had a future together. She would be part of his life forever and create a family with him. A family he'd always wanted.

He lifted his gaze, met her brown eyes and said, "You've made me the happiest man." He inwardly groaned. The words sounded corny but they were true. He loved her and now he had proof that she loved him too. He'd never been certain of it. Until this moment, he still hadn't been sure and knew that asking her to marry him posed a risk. But it had been worth it. He got his confirmation. Someone could love him just the way he was. It was a great feeling.

He heard a soft sigh and then noticed a slight hesitation in her eyes. A sliver of fear crawled up his back. Something was wrong. She didn't look as happy as he'd hoped she would be. He cleared his throat and forced himself to say, "What is it?" He cleared his throat again and resisted the urge to tug on his collar. Something was wrong. She wasn't happy. Had he chosen the wrong ring? The wrong time? Said the wrong thing?

Her mouth softened into a smile. She touched his cheek. "Nothing. I'm...surprised."

"Surprised?"

She nodded. "I wasn't sure you'd ask me."

"Why not?"

She shrugged. "I'm not always sure how you feel about me."

Seriously? She didn't know? He'd always been clear with her. Very clear. As obvious as Optimus Prime was the leader of the Autobots in the Transformers. How more obvious could a man be? There was never another woman in his life. He devoted his free time to her. He was a great lover. He supported her career. He took her out and treated her. Sure, at times, he could be a little obsessive about his work, but he always made sure to give her what time he could. What she said didn't make sense.

Bryant brushed her words aside like he did with most things that didn't make logical sense and had no apparent meaning. Her confusion didn't matter now. She'd agreed to marry him, that's all he needed to know. "Well, now you know how I feel."

"Yes." She looked down at the ring. "It's beautiful."

He knew it was (she had high standards so he had only three options in choosing a ring: beautiful, gorgeous and spectacular. He could only afford "beautiful" at his present salary but he hoped to reach "spectacular" by their fifth year anniversary), he was just glad she liked it.

He folded his arms. Damn. This was supposed to be the happiest day of his life. Why did he still feel on edge? Everything was perfect. The cloudless blue sky on a spring afternoon, the ring, her response and he'd chosen the perfect location. A private gazebo in Howard Park. They were surrounded by the scent of roses drafting towards them, and the bright, happy song of a wren singing in the evergreens.

Only moments before he'd gotten down on one knee, his heart racing, afraid he'd drop the box before he opened it for her. The look on her face (at first he thought she looked horrified, but he was sure he hadn't read her expression right and his worries disappeared when he saw tears in her eyes) had told him that the private location had been best. He wasn't confident she would say yes. He hadn't been the first man to pursue her.

Marlon Scott's second daughter was a worthy prize. But that wasn't what had first attracted him to her. Aside from her looks, mocha skin with big brown eyes, she was smart and he could talk to her. It had taken weeks before she could trust that he wasn't interested in her only to further his career in the company.

And now she would be his wife. *See Dad? I'm not a loser.*

He'd made the right life for himself although it hadn't always been that way. He'd gone from fixing cars to Design Manager at a small toy company that was steadily growing and now he'd have a partner in life to take him further. His father would be shocked and he could imagine his face. His father never thought Bryant's relationship with Esme would last.

"You're aiming too high there," he'd told him after meeting Esme at a family gathering.

"We get on."

His father sniffed. He was a thin, bespectacled man who'd immigrated from Jamaica with the belief that his children should surpass him in academic degrees and profession. He'd been a tenured professor and published author and despaired that neither of his children had managed to get past a bachelor's degree. "You still have grease under your nails."

It was always his father's way to remind him that he hadn't come from money the way Esme had. That he hadn't gone straight to college the way she had. He'd taken a more circuitous route. Sick of his father's put-downs ("You're as thick as banana porridge," was a favorite of his) Bryant hadn't put much effort in school and had barely graduated high school. He'd opened a mobile auto repair business after graduation and had run it for a couple years while secretly taking art classes part time.

When a teacher recommended he try for the Industrial Design Program at the University of Cincinnati he'd hesitated until his father told him he'd fail.

"What do you need a damn art degree for? You barely made it out of high school, why stress yourself? You've got a successful business and have all the skills you need. What will drawing teach you? You're setting yourself up for failure."

Bryant had applied and been accepted into the program just to prove him wrong (and an overwhelming desire to accomplish something more in his life). He didn't fail and he learned more than drawing but also drafting, how to build model depictions of his ideas and much more. He'd eventually landed a co-op job with a toy-making company in his junior year and after five different co-op assignments with the company, they'd hired him once he'd graduated.

Then Hasbro had bought the company and consolidated the workforce. He feared he would find himself floundering, since his job had been made redundant, and when a number of other places turned him down he got nervous. Then he got an offer to move to Virginia and landed at Scott Designs. He rented a house, not sure how long the position would last and slowly rose to the rank of Design Manager with four designers who reported to him.

Esme's father, a former NASA scientist, had developed a game that started his new business, Scott Designs, while in semiretirement and still proved a steady seller fifteen years later. The company also worked with licensures they purchased from independent book publishers and movie projects with loyal, cult followings. It never ceased to amaze him how much a rabid fan was willing to pay for an item from a world they were obsessed about.

However, when Bryant had come on board the company had just suffered a major commercial loss and was struggling. He'd managed to help turn it around, using his experience as a business owner and lessons he'd learned from his work at the other company. While his specialization was action figures and scale models, he'd managed to assist them in developing scientific exploration toys that had become the bedrock of their inventory.

And as the success of the company changed he'd hoped to buy the house he'd been renting for the past four years. It had been on the market without much interest, but when Bryant had gotten sick the owner had briefly taken it off the market only to put it back on when he was well again. But when another year passed and she got no buyers he felt secure it would never sell, until the owner told him she'd sold it and wanted him out by the end of the week. She'd apologized profusely but the house had been on the market so long she'd feared no one would want it.

Bryant left wishing he'd made his interest known, but he had been too late. So six months ago he'd had to quickly find another place—a large room in a house with one other roommate and the owner. It suited as a transitory place and Esme hadn't minded it. Now that they were getting married they could go shopping for a place together since she lived with her parents in their large shingle styled home and he had no intention of staying there despite the size. They'd discuss that later. One step at a time.

He'd proven to his father that he could be a success on his own terms.

He'd proven to Scott Designs that he was a valuable employee.

And he'd proven to Esme that he'd make a great husband.

For the first time Bryant felt like he belonged in the world. He'd achieved all that he'd wanted in life and wanted to celebrate. Something he rarely did.

"My landlord's throwing a party tomorrow night," he said. "Join me?"

"Sure."

Bryant smiled and kissed her again, hoping that soon his heart would stop pounding and the shadow of fear that had followed him most of his thirty-four years would finally disappear.

CHAPTER TWO

She'd rather get her teeth pulled.

Cheryl Whelan hated parties. She was terrible at parties. She thought a party was a stupid idea. But her mother thought it was good to keep the tenants happy. "If you don't want to do this get-together, your sister can."

Cheryl gripped her phone and rolled her eyes. That was her mother's favorite threat, one she'd used on her since she was a child. *If you can't do, it Maddy can. If you can't sell all your Girl Scout cookies Maddy can. If you can't make the dance squad, Maddy can. If you can't host your great-aunt, Maddy can.* And her sister Maddy could. There were few things her older sister—The Doctor—couldn't do. It was as if her parents had given birth to the perfect child and then a giant mistake.

She was the mistake.

An immigrant couple's nightmare. An aggressive, ambitious daughter with a degree in civil engineering who preferred to be behind a backhoe loader or computer rather than host guests at a party and chat about her recent travel to Spain or her summerhouse in North Carolina. But she didn't want to be outshone in her own house and it was *her* house no matter how much the family wanted to act as if it were theirs.

Cheryl mentally counted to ten to make sure she didn't sound angry. "I can do it."

"How many tenants do you have?"

Cheryl inwardly groaned. She didn't want to tell the truth. She knew her mother would start calculating what revenue she was generating. Her mother was a whiz at numbers and a magician when it came to uncovering profit margins. She'd helped her family manage a hotel in her native Nigeria. But lying was also tricky. She had to be sly. "Three."

"Only three?"

"Dexter moved out."

Her mother paused. "Why don't you sell the house to us? It's a large house. Too large for you to manage and with some savvy marketing we can have the place filled and turning a profit within—"

"I run my business from the house. It also showcases what I can do."

"You can take a picture of the house and rent an office space."

"I'll get more housemates."

"Tenants, dear. You're not running a college dorm. Although...you are close to a university, aren't you? You could—"

"I'm not turning it into a place for college students."

"I know and there are a lot of young professionals sharing houses nowadays. The opportunity to—"

"No, Mom."

"If the thought seems overwhelming, we can do this together. If you want to—"

"Everything is fine just the way it is."

"It's not fine. You're not fooling anyone. We all know you need the extra income to help pay the debts you were left with after—"

"I'm taking care of them."

"Cheryl you—"

"The party will be fine," she said in a bright, tight voice. "The food will be fine. I'm fine. Everything's *fine*."

"What caterer are you using?"

Cheryl gave her the name then heard her mother sigh (She could read a lot into that sigh. That sigh meant 'good you won't embarrass us') before she said, "If you need anything—"

"I'll let you know. Bye."

She hung up, wiped her damp hands on her jeans then sat back in her empty living room. She'd lied. She'd only managed to rent two rooms. At first she'd managed four but then one guy left without notice and another woman had stayed briefly then left a week later saying the air was toxic, whatever the heck that meant. She'd left Cheryl with a business card for a service that helped "Clear the emotional toxins that can clutter up one's life."

She should have thrown it away, but she'd found the idea of it so amusing she'd kept the card in a drawer in her office and pulled it out every once in a while when she needed a good giggle.

Cheryl sighed and stared up at the high vaulted ceiling and could imagine her mother eying all the features of the five bedroom, brick colonial situated on a large corner lot, affording privacy and great parking. "It also has a big yard, game/main room, family room, formal living room and gourmet kitchen with the latest appliances, an eating bar, breakfast nook and kitchen island." Cheryl had one guy living in the large master bedroom with its own bath and another woman in a smaller, yet still spacious, room with walk-in closet and private shower. There were two more rooms that could be occupied, but finding other tenants had been tricky.

The truth was that right now she lived with a hermit and killer. Both paid on time but she didn't know much else.

The hermit was a woman. She at least knew that much. Small, with dark circles under her eyes and a raspy voice. But she hardly saw her and only rarely heard her.

The killer...now he was something different entirely. Cheryl always knew when he was around and tried to stay out of his way. Although she couldn't stand him. He'd run over her azaleas. Twice. The ones she'd had a landscaper place along the driveway, the jerk had driven over and killed them. The thought still enraged her. Those brightly colored flowers leading up to the house had been one of Martin's favorite designs...

But she didn't want to focus on that now.

Right now she had to focus on the stupid party.

She'd have to organize the party to include people from her business, Whelan Builders, otherwise her mother would find out the truth about how empty the house really was and she didn't want that. She needed to prove that she could manage the house. That she could manage her life. It was so easy for others to think that she needed to be rescued after what had happened.

But she was independent and capable.

She had rescued herself.

She had moved on.

Now she had to show it.

CHAPTER THREE

*I*t was definitely a rock. And for some strange reason she felt as if it were drowning her.

Esme gazed down at her engagement ring conflicted. It really was beautiful. The sight of it had literally taken her breath away and made her heart skip a beat. If only the man could do the same. She really liked Bryant. He was attractive enough, definitely talented (he still amazed her by all he was able to do) and he'd saved her father's company, although he was too polite to admit it (he was also too polite to admit that she was the cause that the business had nearly gone into bankruptcy because of bad management), but...she wasn't sure she loved him.

She wasn't sure he was the kind of a man a woman could love. He was like a brick.

A solid brick.

A brick had its uses. It could be used to build or as a weapon. One would notice if it was out of place or missing, but one didn't fall in love with a brick.

Or did they? What was love anyway? Bryant could give her a nice stable life. He was familiar. Her father approved. Her mother approved. Everyone approved.

It was the right thing to do. That's why she'd said yes. The only reason really. It felt like it was part of the script. She felt as if her entire life had been scripted and she'd been playing her part so well, and for so long, she'd forgotten she was playing a role anymore. *Stick to the script and nothing could go wrong.*

But she had almost forgotten that. Bryant had surprised her. Shocked her, if she was being truly honest. Bryant, her brick, had always been reliable, predictable. His proposal had felt as if it had come out of nowhere. Perhaps she hadn't paid close enough attention. Usually a woman could sense a moment like this coming, but Bryant wasn't an easy man to read. Never had been and she never imagined he was thinking about marriage. He seemed the kind of man who could happily live alone the rest of his life with a dash of great sex here and there.

And that was what bothered her. He was far from domestic. He could pretend, but it never felt real. He didn't seem completely real. He was like a deep ocean with layers she didn't know. And she liked to know things. She didn't like surprises. She liked staying on script. She liked understanding the full scope of everything, but Bryant remained a mystery even after two years. What would he be like as a husband? What script was she supposed to follow then?

She bit her thumbnail and felt a sharp kick in the shins. She winced, placed her hand back in her lap and glanced up at the mirror image of herself twenty-some years in the future (a little thicker in the middle with expertly cut natural gray hair). Esme had come straight home from the park (instead of wandering around in a daze, trying to make sense of how she really felt) to tell her mother about Bryant's proposal. That action was part of the script as well and she'd followed it flawlessly, showing her mother the ring and sharing the news.

"I thought you'd gotten out of that habit," her mother said.

Esme had stopped biting her nails years ago. She hadn't realized she'd started again. "I'm sorry. I'm a little nervous."

"No reason to be. You did well," her mother said with a satisfied nod. That was glowing praise from a woman who rarely offered it. "He's exactly the kind of man you need."

"I didn't realize I needed a man."

Her mother narrowed her eyes. "Sarcasm doesn't become you."

Oops. She'd gone off-script, that wasn't like her. "I wasn't being sarcastic."

"Neither does cheekiness."

"I'm sorry." And she truly was. She didn't know what had gotten into her. She'd made her mother happy. Her father would be happy too. Wasn't that enough?

"What's wrong?" her mother said.

"I didn't say anything was wrong."

Her mother pursed her lips. "You didn't need too. It's all over your face. I hope you were able to school your features when you were with him."

She inwardly sighed. She hadn't. Bryant had read her

too (she remembered the confusion in his voice), but her mother didn't need to know that. "Of course I did. Bryant's happy." At least that was true.

"Then tell me what's wrong."

Esme glanced down at the ring again. Her mother cared about her but she was not one Esme would choose to confide in. She always blocked out what she didn't want to hear. "It's just unexpected, I guess."

"It's long overdue if you ask me. One year should have been sufficient. But you can't pressure a man like Bryant so your patience was perfect. At least you weren't as silly as your sister, giving a man eight years before he made up his mind."

"They're happy and they—"

"It could have been time wasted. By year seven he could have grown tired of her and dashed off with someone else. Stupid girl."

"But she—"

"Thank goodness you have more sense. You understand the importance of management." She struck the flat of her palm with her fist. "Time must be utilized." She pointed at Esme. "And when it comes to a woman remember you're always on the clock."

"You don't have to make it sound so clinical."

"You know what I mean. There's no need to be precious about a harsh reality. You have your looks and your fertility, it's a marketplace out there and you're in a fierce competition. Not just locally but globally." She lowered her voice. "The Robertson's son is marrying a woman from Canada."

"That's not exactly half way around the world."

"My point is that there are a lot of woman out there and you're not getting any younger—"

"Thank goodness. I wouldn't want to be in diapers again and I don't think teething was much fun either."

Her mother's eyes narrowed again. She didn't move and she didn't reply. She just stared at Esme for one very long moment making her displeasure clear. "You're in a mood," she finally said in a quiet voice.

Esme took a deep, steadying breath. *Stay on script. Tell her what she wants to hear.* "I'm sorry. I guess...I'm still in shock."

"This is great news."

She nodded feeling like a puppet. "Yes. It's done. I'm engaged to Bryant. You don't have to worry anymore. I'll get married, have a family and happily continue the business."

Her mother flashed a brief smile. "Good. Now repeat that and mean it."

CHAPTER FOUR

"Um...do you even know half of these people?" Cheryl whispered to the tall man beside her as they stood in the formal living room staring at the festive crowd. Shawn Whelan was her business partner and brother-in-law.

Shawn couldn't stop a smile, his white teeth emerging through his trim black beard. He was a good looking man, built just the way she liked a man—big like a truck, strong like an ox—with an easy laugh. He worked as a contractor. "I got a little carried away. I wanted to make sure there were enough people."

"If there were any more people we'd have to get an adjoining tent."

"You'd know how to build it."

She shot him a look. "Was that supposed to be an apology?"

"Has your mother bothered you?"

She curled her lip.

"Was that a thank you, BB Cream?" he said, using her nickname.

She'd gotten it years ago when she'd arrived early to a construction site and one of her colleagues had caught her applying moisturizer and BB Cream to her face (hey she knew what cold and wind could do to a woman's complexion) before she got out of her car. When he'd asked her what it was and she told him, he'd used it as her nickname throughout the rest of the job and it had stuck. Shawn liked to use it to annoy her, but she kissed him on the cheek anyway. "Thank you."

"That's more like it." He turned and tapped his other cheek.

She kissed it as well. He tapped his lips. She playfully shoved him away. "Don't push it."

He shrugged. "I did save you."

He wasn't far from wrong, she wouldn't have managed to pull off the event without him. "Thanks for coming."

"Free food. Pretty women. Your depthless thanks. You'd think I'd pass that up?"

"I'm also hoping I can get some names for people interested in renting a room."

"I thought there might be an alternative motive for this fiasco. Who haven't you scared off yet?"

She shot him another look. "I haven't scared anybody."

Shawn folded his arms. "Who's left?"

She sighed. "Enough."

Shawn's brows shot up. "How many is enough?"

"Two."

"You only have *two* renters in this place?"

She nudged him with her elbow. "Shh."

"You once had five."

"Four."

"And you terrified two. How did you manage that?"

"It's complicated." She glanced away. "At least they pay on time."

"But you don't like them," Shawn said in a knowing voice.

"I hardly know the woman, but the guy is a nuisance. Ran over my azaleas twice."

"I know you told me."

"The first time I could take as a mistake, the second time was definitely deliberate. Jerk. Flower killer. Plant predator."

"You don't know that."

"I know that if I could get two more housemates I'd tell him to leave."

"Over plants? Did you ask him to pay for the damages?"

"Yes...actually no. He offered, but it doesn't matter. Something about him bothers me. Even when I first met him, I shouldn't have let him stay."

"Well, at least he hasn't killed any other plants and the party is working so stop worrying and try to enjoy yourself." Shawn bent down, his warm breath teasing her ear, and whispered. "Now I'm going to mingle."

Cheryl watched him leave and catch the attention of two women she'd never seen before. She sipped her drink. *Enjoy yourself.* Easier said than done. This house hadn't seen so many people since their housewarming party and that had been...

She finished her drink and set the glass aside. No use thinking about the past. She scanned the crowd to see if there was anyone to talk to when her gaze caught sight of him.

Bryant Hill.

She felt her temper ignite. He was Shawn and Martin's complete opposite. Tough and lean. She hadn't expected him to show up. The hermit had appeared for twenty minutes before scuttling back into her room and Cheryl had guessed that he wouldn't have arrived until the party was nearly over. He wasn't the party type. He didn't mingle, he didn't joke. He even looked bored. Why was he there? It wasn't as if he was doing her a favor.

"Great party," a woman said beside her.

Cheryl turned with a polite remark on her lips then stopped. The woman was perfection. Beautiful, poised. Had she gotten lost on the way to somewhere else? She was the kind of woman who made Cheryl feel like a stubby, husky girl in her pressed dark blue trousers and yellow blouse. It wasn't the other woman's fault she ignited Cheryl's insecurities. She had to think like Maddy. Be charming not intimidated.

She plastered on a smile, hoping it didn't look antiseptic. "Thanks."

The woman looked at her then at Bryant. "Are you interested in him?"

Cheryl jerked her head back as if the other woman had spit on her. "What?! Wh-why would you think that?"

"Because you keep looking at him."

"He's like watching a car crash. You want to look away but you can't. No," she said with a shudder. "I have absolutely no interest in him. I couldn't imagine any sane woman could."

The woman furrowed her perfect brows. "Why would you think that?"

Cheryl didn't know why the woman's attention flattered her but it did. It was rare that she mingled with women like her, let alone had them listening to her and she felt like showing off and entertaining her. Plus discussing the flaws of Bryant Hill was one of her favorite topics. "Aside from the fact that he looks like a man with no pulse? I mean it's a party, what's with the black? Is he supposed to be Death? Actually that's true he is a killer."

"A killer?"

"Yes," Cheryl said then told her about the azaleas.

The woman released a nervous giggle. "He's good looking though."

Cheryl shook her head with a frown. "That's even worse."

"Worse?"

"Yes, a guy like that is used to using his looks. He doesn't even try to be charming because he doesn't have to be. If some woman was stupid enough to fall for him they'd find out fast how much he's not what he seems."

"Really?" the woman asked, sounding more thoughtful than surprised.

"Yes. Count on it. Although he rents here, I try my best to keep my distance. He's too cold for my taste, I bet you he has a controlling streak. I once moved one of his shoes just a little out of the way and you would have thought I'd committed a crime."

"Yes," the woman said sounding grim. "He has his moments."

Cheryl paused. A flicker of apprehension shot through her. "You know him?"

The woman smiled. "Vaguely."

"He's probably not single, but if he is I'd look elsewhere." Cheryl lowered her voice and looked around. "I'm even worried he might have an unhealthy interest in children."

"Unhealthy?"

"I would hate to think he's a pedophile, but I've never seen a single man hang out with kids the way he does. I have a hermit...excuse me...a woman who lives here and he hangs out with her daughter. A grown man with a little girl." She sent the woman a pointed look. "If that isn't shady I don't know what is. The kid seems to like him and maybe that says something. He watches lots of kids movies and I once saw him playing with Play-Doh by himself."

"Hmm."

"But I'm not one to gossip so... Oh no, I caught his eye. Damn, he's coming this way. Don't look at him and maybe he'll leave us alone."

But her hopes were dashed when he stopped in front of them. It was likely her companion who had caught his interest. A woman like her probably got lots of attention.

"What are you two talking about?" he asked.

"I was complimenting her on the party," the woman

said. She held out her hand to Cheryl. "I'm sorry I didn't introduce myself. I'm Esme Scott."

"Cheryl Whelan." She looked at Bryant. "And this is—"

"I already know who he is."

Her faint apprehension from before grew slowly into dread. "You do?"

"Yes," Bryant said with a cool smile. "She's my fiancée."

Cheryl felt all blood leave her face. No. no. Please tell me I misheard him. "Y-your fiancée?"

"Yes."

Cheryl managed to look at Esme's composed features. *You cruel woman. You got me.*

But Esme grinned back with a secret expression as if to say Don't worry, I won't tell him a thing. Your secret is safe with me. "It was nice chatting with you."

Chatting? She was sneaky, gathering intelligence. She'd set Cheryl up, and was probably laughing behind her back. She shouldn't have trusted her. She deserved him. Cheryl watched the couple walk away, wishing the floor would open up and swallow her.

CHAPTER FIVE

Could a heart literally break?

Could it literally split into two and stop beating?

Bryant stared at the engagement ring on the square wooden table in disbelief. They'd decided to have lunch at a nearby bistro that served Filipino classics. Her idea, not his. That should have been his first clue something was wrong. She never instigated time alone with him on a weekday. He looked at her barely touched spring roll.

No, no, no this was all wrong. This couldn't be happening. Esme Scott couldn't be telling him that she was sorry, that it wouldn't work between them. That she couldn't marry him. Only three days ago they'd been happy, right?

Bryant took a deep breath. Calm and controlled. He needed to be calm and controlled not overexcited. He needed to be understanding. Something had spooked her that was all. He'd figure out what it was and then every-thing would be back to normal.

He reached over the table and touched her hand. "What's wrong?"

She pulled her hand away. "I just told you. It has nothing to do with you."

Pain swept through him. No matter what she said, how nicely she said it, all he heard was "You're not good enough and I don't love you."

"You are an amazing guy. And I thought I could marry you. I wanted to marry you, but after talking to her —" She shook her head. "Never mind."

Bryant felt his heart grow cold. Something hadn't spooked her, *someone* had. Somebody had come into his life and tried to steal what he'd fought to gain. He wouldn't let that happen so easily. "Who was it? Your mother?"

"No," Esme said with a sour laugh. "It wasn't her. You know my mother adores you. As much as she can adore anyone."

He felt a little tension ebb. He'd worked hard to win over Esme's parents and that was no small feat. Mrs. Scott was even more critical than his father had been. But someone else had influenced Esme and convinced her to change her mind about him. That person was his enemy and that enemy would be defeated. All he needed was a name. "Who was it?"

She glanced down at the small, black box on the table. "Bryant...just take the ring back."

"Who was it?"

"The point isn't who—"

"Yes, it is. Tell me who changed your mind about me. Shouldn't the accused know their accuser?"

Esme looked embarrassed. "It wasn't really her fault, I wasn't sure about our relationship and she...she made me see things a little clearer."

Esme had doubted their relationship? What was there to doubt? He'd been clear. He'd always been clear. But he wouldn't get angry. *Calm and controlled.* He had to stay cool. "Who?"

Esme shook her head and inched the box closer to him. "It won't change anything."

He waited, resisting the urge to grab the box and hide it away. It wasn't just a little box on the table; it was his heart being rejected. But he couldn't touch it until he understood more about why she couldn't marry him after everything he'd done for her. "Please tell me who."

"I don't want you getting mad at her."

Her. The mysterious *her.* He didn't care who *she* was. He already imagined dragging her through hot coals. He folded his arms, pleased to keep his tone neutral. "Who did you talk to?"

"Your landlord...uh lady."

His arms fell, he stared at her stunned. "My landlord?"

"Yes. Your landlady."

"Lord," he corrected. "Do you know why I call her that? Because she told me to. She told me that 'landlord' had a more dignified and respectable ring to it. It was more gender neutral."

"I see."

"That respect means a lot to her."

"You're getting angry."

He was way passed angry, but he'd never let that show. "What could she possibly know about me?"

"More than you think."

"I've hardly spoken to the woman." He couldn't even remember her name. He had his payment set up for automatic deposits. She'd told Esme her name at the party, but he'd quickly forgotten it. It started with an S or something.

"Like I said, it's not her fault. It's mine and I—"

"Esme, it's a big decision to make and I know that. I know that you're wavering, but saying yes to me the other day was the right thing. Don't let some demented stranger come between us."

"She's not demented."

"You're standing up for her now?"

Esme picked up the box and held it out to him. "I'm sorry. I really am."

He wouldn't take it. He refused to take it. Bryant looked out the window at a well-dressed couple passing by, looking happy like how he and Esme used to be. He watched them wishing Esme knew how much she was hurting him by returning his ring. Holding out his heart and dreams for the world to see. "What did she say?"

"It's not the specifics that matter—"

He shifted his gaze to her. "If my landlord is trash talking about me behind my back I have a right to know." He saw Esme wince and realized he'd come on too strong. *Stay calm and controlled, Bryant.* "What did she say?"

Esme sighed resigned and set the box down. "Well, for one thing..."

He stopped listening after five minutes. Two long minutes of criticism from a woman he barely knew. As Esme continued to speak the anger within him gathered fuel until he didn't hear any words, only the roaring in his head and in front of him Esme's face disappeared.

He only saw her face. The face of his enemy, his nemesis. His Megatron, Jafar, Scar. The villain that had to be defeated.

Bryant grabbed the small box and shoved it in his coat pocket. He would get his revenge.

CHAPTER SIX

She'd always pictured Death with a scythe not a set of keys.

Cheryl had prepared for the moment. Dreaded it. Feared it. She'd hardly been able to sleep the past couple days. Silently pleading that Esme wouldn't let Bryant know what she'd said about him. When he hadn't mentioned anything for two days she'd started to relax.

Perhaps Esme was someone she could trust. Perhaps she'd just been teasing her and would keep her secret safe.

She'd been wrong.

Very wrong from the look on Bryant's face and she didn't know what to do. She sat behind her office desk and gripped her hands in her lap. She'd never seen a man so angry. If he could hurt her, perhaps rip her in two, he would have, but fortunately she knew he had more control than that.

But she had to stop him. He couldn't leave. She

couldn't end up with only one tenant. That would just be pitiful and expensive. She needed the income. Her husband's illness had wiped out all their savings and investments and left her drowning in debt.

If only she hadn't tried to impress that woman by sounding clever and she'd kept her big mouth shut. Perhaps if she pretended not to know why he was upset that would smooth things over. Maybe there was another reason he was upset, there was no need to jump to conclusions. She stared at the keys and blinked. "What are you doing?"

He gently placed his set of house keys on her desk. That action surprised her. She'd expected him to drop them or throw them. He folded his arms and waited.

"You're leaving. You don't need to do that. I thought you were happy." Happy was the wrong choice of words. He looked content before, not happy. He wasn't the kind of man to look happy.

He turned and walked to the door. There was no mention of his deposit that meant he didn't care. That was really bad news for her. She had to stop him. She jumped to her feet.

"There must be a misunderstanding."

He stopped. "A misunderstanding?"

It was the first time he'd spoken since he'd entered her office. His voice made her think of coffins and candle-light and graveyards at night. She held back a shiver. "Yes." He'd stopped walking, that's what she needed to focus on. Not the fact that he made her nervous. She needed him to turn around and sit down.

"You think I came in here because of a misunderstanding?" he said, keeping his back towards her.

She wiped her damp hands on her jeans. "It's possible. Let's talk."

"Yes." He spun on his heel and faced her, his dark eyes piercing hers. "Let's."

He wasn't leaving, but Cheryl didn't feel any better. In fact part of her wanted to shove him out the door and say, "Fine go. I'd wanted to get rid of you anyway." But another part saw Shawn's smug face saying, "You scared him off too? Sure you don't want to sell the house?" This man was more than just a tenant he was her chance to prove herself. Prove that she could make a mistake and fix it on her own. This was her house, her office. She held the power in this domain. She returned to her desk.

He sat down, his gaze filled with challenge. "Go ahead. Tell me you didn't tell my fiancée not to marry me."

"I didn't know you had a fiancée."

"So you did talk about me."

"In a roundabout way."

He nodded. "I see."

"I was a little tipsy and annoyed."

He fell silent a moment then said, "You're still pissed about your stupid bushes?"

She counted to five. "They aren't bushes. They're—"

"I apologized."

"Then you ran over them again. How does someone make the same mistake twice?"

"I offered to pay." He shook his head. "I can't believe we're arguing about this again. Keep the damn deposit.

I'm gone and you and your damn *bushes* don't have to worry about me anymore."

He stood.

She jumped to her feet. If he left he'd be taking his regular monthly payments with him. She shouldn't have let him provoke her. He had a right to be upset. She had to keep her temper in check and make him feel better. "Wait. I'm sorry. I wish it hadn't happened."

He rested his hands on his hips. "And I wish strangling wasn't a crime."

"I understand you're upset."

He held her gaze and lowered his voice to an ominous purr. "No, I'm not upset. I'm way past upset. Right now I'm very angry."

"But I didn't mean..." She threw up her hands in frustration. "This is all so silly."

"I'm glad you find it amusing."

Wrong choice of words. She needed to change tactics. Not insult him, but maybe if she let him see how she had helped him he wouldn't be so upset. "Let's look at this in a different way. I did you a favor. If she really loved you it wouldn't have been so easy to change her mind. You're better off without her."

He didn't move.

He didn't blink.

She wasn't even sure he was breathing.

She had a sinking feeling she was making things worse. "Never mind that. I'll—"

He turned. "Goodbye."

She rushed in front of him. "No, don't go. We haven't finished talking."

He leaned towards her, his eyes cold. "I think we have."

She swallowed. She'd never been this close to him before and never hoped to be again. But she wouldn't move an inch until she convinced him to stay. "I'll let you stay a month for free."

"No."

She held up two fingers and waved them in his face. "Two months but that's my final offer."

He pushed her aside.

She grabbed his arm and a fissure of heat coursed through her both from surprise (he was more muscularly built than he looked) and wariness (when he turned to her his dark gaze made it clear he didn't like being touched). "Please just listen—"

His voice turned to ice. "Don't touch me and I won't touch you."

It was the only warning she needed. She quickly let go and held her hands up in surrender. "I'll talk to her."

"You've done enough talking."

"I know and I shouldn't have." She pressed her hands together. "I'm sorry. I truly am. I'll smooth this over for you, I promise. And when I do, all I ask is for you to complete your one year rental here." When he didn't reply she added, "I'll also give you a month free as a wedding present."

He nodded. "Fine. I'll give you two days."

A reprieve. It was something. Her confidence returned. "Give me her number and I'll repair everything in one."

What the hell was wrong with him? Bryant paced his room. He should have walked away like he planned. Why had he listened to her? Why had she gotten him to stay longer than he should have? He stopped pacing and stared at the black box on his dresser.

Because she'd given him hope. He wanted to believe that she could talk to Esme and fix things. She'd made this mess and she should fix it. He wanted to believe that it was all a misunderstanding and not something worse.

He was desperate.

He hated being desperate.

But he didn't want to face the truth. That Esme didn't love him, maybe never did. That she'd said yes out of pity and had come to her senses and realized that she couldn't be with him. It hurt too much to think he hadn't succeeded in winning her heart. That he wasn't the man for her.

That he might not be the right man for anyone.

You're a loser. Who would put up with you?

He closed his eyes. He wasn't a loser. He would get Esme back. He grabbed his keys and headed for the door. He needed to go for a drive.

As he headed down the hall he felt a new sense of determination. He'd put his ring back on Esme's finger. Two days. He'd given that woman two days. In two days she'd seal her fate and his own.

CHAPTER SEVEN

The Kents were straight out of a Hallmark movie. After being threatened by the Grim Reaper (otherwise known as Bryant Hill who she had to reunite with his lady love in two days...argh) they were a welcome alternative. A young, black couple with perfect teeth, hair, clothes and an adorable infant as cute as a plush toy. Cheryl could give them a perfect history to go with their perfect image. They had met by accident at a local coffee shop—their orders had gotten mixed up—and haven't been separated since. He was a rising doctor and she was a political science major who had taken time off to raise their child. They'd live their charmed life on the property the woman had inherited from her great uncle and live happily ever after.

At least the house was interesting. Otherwise they were so sweet it was slightly sickening. Cheryl had loved her husband but they'd never looked like this. Perhaps it was jealousy. They'd have the happy ending she'd once wished for.

The fairytale couple had hired Cheryl to build their new house and had come to her office to talk about the plans.

"And you've done other homes like this before?" Mrs. Kent asked, a note of unease in her tone.

Cheryl held back a sigh. *Thanks for the vote of confidence, sister. No, this is my first,* Cheryl wanted to say with an impish grin. It always amazed her that she got more questions from the women who hired her than the men. So much for girl power. But she knew she was an anomaly in the field. There had been few women in her engineering course and even fewer (hardly any) when she worked three years as a construction engineer at building sites. She got a lot of stares when she took off her helmet, which had been rare. But despite the biases that came with her chosen profession she still loved it.

She loved building things. She still remembered the thrill she'd received as a child when she convinced her babysitter to let her watch a structure get built. Other kids played on the swings or went to the zoo. She watched in awe as tons of soil lifted into the air and giggled with joy at the roar of earth moving equipment like a backhoe loader or bulldozer eat up the ground and fell in love with an excavator. She saw herself doing nothing else.

She'd met Martin on a job six years ago. He had been one of the subcontractors and owned a business with his brother. She never would have imagined marrying another engineer but they blended well together. It seemed fitting to go into business together and she didn't mind using her married surname, Whelan, to get Whelan Builders off the ground expanding the brother's subcontractor business into larger projects.

When Martin got sick he begged her to keep the company going. Afraid she'd hand it over to someone else. She assured him that it was something they'd built together and she'd never let it go. Just like the house. She'd keep his memory alive.

"But I don't want you living in the past," he'd said, his voice weak from various medications as he lay in his hospital bed. He'd lost forty pounds off his six-one frame, but his words were firm.

Cheryl sat by the side of his bed and held his hand. "I won't."

"I want you to keep building things. It's what you love."

Tears burned her eyes and tightened her throat. "I love you. And if I could build anything it would be a time machine so that I could fast forward to another century where medicine was more advanced and they could heal you."

He sighed, the effort seeming to shake his entire body. "I love you too. And you can make a time machine in a way because a new building or structure always represents the future. It's about possibilities and progress and changing lives." He lifted his hand and cupped her face. "That's why I want you to keep the company going. I want you to build things thinking about the future. *Your* future."

Cheryl rested her cheek against his large, calloused

hand, but didn't respond. She didn't want to think about a future without him.

"Promise me," he whispered.

She couldn't make that promise. She couldn't promise that she would remain unchanged, that building things would give her the same joy it once had. So she took his hand and tenderly kissed it instead before she told him to go to sleep.

When he died no one fought her about taking his place. Their present clients and contractors knew her capabilities but gaining trust from others remained a struggle, because based on their reputation most outsiders still thought Martin had been the one behind the company's success. And those in the general public still felt more comfortable dealing with a male, which was why she hadn't taken his voice off the message machine and still kept his email account open.

Once new clients met her and realized she'd be in charge of the project she faced another obstacle—gaining their trust. Like the couple she faced now. They'd agreed to work with her based on a glowing referral, but their apprehension was still present, hers more than his.

"We've seen your work," Mr. Kent said, sounding a little embarrassed by his wife's question.

"It's just a question," his wife snapped back. "It's a big job." She looked at Cheryl. "Are you sure you know what you're doing?"

Cheryl forced a reassuring smile. She'd learned to be patient with clients. But she was tempted to say, "No, since my Barbie playhouse fell to the ground, I've lost most of my confidence but I'm willing to try." Or better yet "The dung hut I helped my grandmother build is still standing so I think so." But Martin had taught her how to take hold of her temper. That's initially why she'd liked working out in the field, getting the job done, seeing her effort come to something, instead of stroking the egos of people who were more ignorant of the process than they pretended to be.

She remembered one afternoon practicing her smile with Martin after a meeting with a prospect hadn't gone well. They sat in the living room with a half eaten Mexican takeaway meal. "No, that's too sweet," he said, critiquing her expression. "Try not to smile too wide or they will think that you don't know what you're doing. A soft smile without teeth, but not condescending."

Cheryl tried what he said, but threw up her hands in frustration when he started to laugh. "It's too hard. I'm not good warming up clients. I'll stay in the background, the brains behind the brawn, you deal with them."

"But what if I'm busy with another job? Besides you know more about building construction than I do. You're in charge of our large projects. I won't always be around, you need to learn this."

Little did he know how true his words would be. Cheryl inwardly sighed, keeping her practiced smile in place and said, "Yes, I am certain that you and your family will be in a home you will be proud of. I can give you more references if you need."

"That won't be necessary," Mr. Kent said.

Mrs. Kent pointed to the blueprint. "We want another room to adjoin this one."

"If you make it a separate bedroom with its own bath you will increase your resale value," Cheryl said.

The woman lifted a brow. "Resale value?"

"Yes, the amount you could charge in case you want to sell."

"Why would we ever want to do that? This is our dream house. We haven't even built it yet and you're talking about selling it?"

Cheryl kept his voice calm. "Please don't misunderstand me. I know you may intend to stay there forever—"

Mrs. Kent's voice thinned. "We *will* stay there forever."

"But unexpected life events can happen," Cheryl continued, determined to make the couple understand. "Such as a new job, or divorce or death. Trust me. I speak from experience. The unforeseen can happen and it's best to—"

Mrs. Kent looked at Cheryl's hand. She could feel the woman's gaze on her now bare ring finger. "Divorced, huh?"

"Widowed."

The other woman's tone softened a fraction as did her gaze. "I see. I'm sorry, but that explains a lot. You're very bitter." She glanced down at her baby, looked adoringly at her husband then returned her gaze to Cheryl. "But we're not. We're building our dream home and we want to know if you're the right person to do that for us."

"I am. I can add an adjoining room."

"And we want a special lightning design for the kitchen."

Cheryl nodded, relieved the woman was still willing

to work with her. "I know of a subcontractor who can handle that."

"Good." They discussed some other minor plans, Cheryl calmly answering every question and increasing their trust in her, before they left.

The moment they were gone she rested her head on her desk and swore. She'd nearly blown it. Two major mistakes in one week. What was wrong with her?

Mrs. Kent was right, what did she care about the resale value? Let them make the decisions they wanted. They were exactly the kind of clients she wanted. She'd once turned down a couple who'd wanted their house in the shape of a cube. She was too traditional for that and particular on what projects she'd attach her name to.

But when had she shifted from offering advice to sounding bitter? So she'd been unlucky, that didn't mean they would be. They would have nothing to ever bother them. Yes, she envied them, but she had to keep that to herself.

"I'm still not sure about her," Cheryl heard Mrs. Kent say through her opened window.

She lifted her head.

"You were fine with this before and she answered all our questions."

Cheryl crept to the window to hear more. She peeked out and saw them settling the baby in the backseat.

"But you heard those awful things she said. Who talks like that about divorce and death?"

"She lost her husband."

"I know but...does she have to look like that?"

Cheryl turned away from the window and touched her cheeks. *Like what? What did she look like?*

"I'm sure she was just trying to give us good advice."

"You're just standing up for her because she's kind of pretty."

Kind of?

She heard a car door close. "That's not it," Mr. Kent said. "You said you were fine with this."

"You won't regret it," a familiar voice said.

Cheryl spun back to the window and saw Bryant. "Her work is top notch. You want a home that will grow with you then this builder is the way to go. And I'm not just saying that because I'm co-owner."

She stared amazed (The guy hated her. Why was he standing up for her?) and glad (He was the male reassurance they needed) and perplexed (Why lie about being co-owner?). He said something else to them in a low voice that she couldn't overhear before they got in their car and drove away. He glanced at the window and tipped an imaginary cap.

She walked down the hall to the foyer to meet him. "Why did you do that?"

"I didn't want you ruining someone else's life."

"I don't know what they said, but I was trying to help them. What else did you say to them?"

He headed for the stairs. "You should be thanking me. And you should learn how to smile."

She followed him. "I did smile at them. Did they say I didn't smile?"

He turned to her. "I mean a real smile."

"My references should speak for me."

"But a smile can always help."

"I was never good at pretending."

"It took them three years to get pregnant."

"How did you find that out?"

"I asked the right question and then I listened. I didn't assume."

He got her there. She had only seen them as the perfect couple. She hadn't thought that life may have thrown them a few curveballs.

"She's nervous about things not going right," Bryant continued, "and doesn't need your pessimism."

"I was being realistic," Cheryl grumbled, annoyed that he was also right about that.

"Sometimes people need you to sell them a dream."

"Dreams die."

He nodded. "Maybe some, but most last forever unless you forget them." His voice turned hard. "And I'm the kind of man who holds onto his dreams. And I won't watch my dream die no matter how hard I have to fight to keep it alive."

Cheryl lowered her gaze unable to meet his. Not because of the anger she saw in his eyes, but the pain. She knew he was talking about Esme. Embarrassment and shame washed over her. Didn't he know how much of his heart he was showing her? He should guard himself better. She didn't want to see him as human.

She cleared her throat and cautiously raised her gaze. "I will get Esme back for you."

"I know. That's also why I helped you." He held her gaze. "Now you owe me even more."

CHAPTER EIGHT

"Can I start laughing now?"

"It's not funny," Cheryl said. She'd returned to her office to find Shawn working on his laptop. When he looked at her face and asked her what was wrong she told him about Bryant now she wondered if she should have. "This is serious."

"You just pissed off one of the last paying tenants in this house and I'm not even allowed a chuckle?"

"He's not the last. I told you there's one more."

"Is that something to brag about? Two tenants in a house this size? You—"

"I can manage."

"Why won't you just admit defeat? Let him leave. Sell the house to your parents and—"

She pulled out her cell phone to see if she had any more appointments. "No."

"You're being stubborn, BB Cream."

She scrolled through her calendar. "No."

"This was bound to happen anyway."

She looked sharply up at him. "What do you mean?"

He sent her a cautious look. "You really want to know?"

"Yes. I made a mistake. That was all. You're making it sound like it's a habit."

"Was it a mistake that you've not been able to keep anyone here?"

"People can be picky and things change."

"People too."

"What's that supposed to mean?"

"You have to admit that you've changed since—"

"No, I haven't. How have I changed?"

Shawn sighed with regret. "You've gotten mean."

"I was just shooting off at the mouth and I admit I was wrong but I don't know why that guy is mad at me."

"That guy?"

"Bryant. The Plant Killer. He should be mad at *her*. Miss Elegant Beauty. If some woman said bad things about the man I loved I'd stand up for him, not break off our engagement. She's weak. I saved them both heartache."

His voice turned sad. "Because love is heartache, right? That's what Martin taught you?"

She shook her head. "Don't bring him into this."

"I don't have to. The sister-in-law I knew wouldn't have said what you did. You're living in the house you two built together and you're not enjoying one square inch. Instead you're chasing people away, working all hours and becoming bitter."

His words stung. She turned away. "I'm not bitter."

"You said love is heartache."

"I didn't you did."

"But you don't believe in it anymore."

"What does that have to do with anything?"

"I loved him too. He was my younger brother. When he passed it hurt, but—"

"But what?" she snapped. "I'm honoring his memory, aren't I? I'm working with you at the business we started together. This has nothing to do with him. What happened at the party has nothing to do with Martin, this house or my past. It's simply people being stupid. Fools for love."

Shawn looked at her for a long moment then said, "How are you going to make someone fall in love again when you don't believe in love anymore?"

"Why do you keep turning my words around? This isn't about me. It's about Bryant's fiancée."

"Former."

She sent him a hooded glance. "She will be his fiancée again. She must have felt something for him at some point. All I have to do is figure out what she saw in him, what traits drew her to him and then remind her of them."

"You sound like your looking over the blueprints of a house."

"Love can be carefully built. It's happened before."

"It can also be messy."

Cheryl shrugged. "The truth is he loves her more than she loves him. He found that out and he wants someone to blame. It's as simple as that. I'll talk to her and then everything will be fine."

"You always say that."

"What?"

"That everything's fine. But I don't believe you."

She opened her laptop. "Don't you have somewhere to be?"

"I've got good news for you. I just secured a major job that should take a few weeks. I'm redesigning a closet the size of this room."

Cheryl looked around the space and gave a low whistle imaging what the price tag on the job could be. "Well done."

"Thank you."

Outside they heard a car door close then a child's voice scream in delight. Cheryl went to the window and saw Bryant hugging a little girl who had a big smile on her face. He waved at the black man who stood on the other side of the car before he took the girl's hand and led her inside.

She didn't know what to think of a man whose best friend seemed to be an eight-year-old girl. The hermit trusted him with her daughter, why should she care? The girl seemed to love being with him. Whenever she caught them together in the game room she overheard them talking with enthusiasm about trips to the park, toy store, and arcade. He seemed to be a big kid. Dressed in black. How the kid didn't find him intimidating she didn't know. Did he lure her with sweets?

Cheryl mentally shook her head and turned from the window. She didn't care. She had nothing to prove to him. She had bigger things to worry about and one was trying to convince a woman who looked like a queen that a humorless man, who dressed all in black, played with kids and killed plants would make a good husband.

CHAPTER NINE

She'd expected flowers. Maybe chocolates, but Esme never expected Bryant's landlady to call her up and request a meeting to plead his case. She was faintly amused. She didn't know how Bryant had convinced her to do this, but he could be persuasive when he wanted to be.

Esme watched the other woman enter the coffee shop, search around then smile in relief when she spotted her. She made her way to the corner booth with desperation in her gaze. She looked terrified. Had Bryant threatened her? No, that wasn't his style, but he'd somehow gotten to her and made her nervous. Esme could understand. He sometimes made her nervous too.

Cheryl collapsed into a seat and spoke in a rush, "Thanks for seeing me. I know that you're busy so I'll keep it short. I'm here because—"

Esme held up her hand wanting to put the poor

woman out of her misery. "Why don't you order something?"

"No, thanks. I'm fine. I really want to discuss—"

"I know why you're here and you don't have to feel bad. You freed me."

Cheryl shook her head. "No, I didn't. Bryant has his good points and—"

"Name five."

She paused, startled. Esme stifled a laugh. She knew she was being a little mean, but couldn't help herself. Teasing Cheryl was too easy.

"Five things?" Cheryl repeated.

Esme nodded.

"But you know him better than I do."

"That's the problem. I'm not sure I do. Don't worry, he'll get over it."

"He really cares about you."

"Then why didn't he come here to say so himself?"

Cheryl hesitated before she said, "He will, I only wanted to say my piece first. How long were you two together?"

"Two years."

"And that means something sp—"

"Two years," Esme interrupted in a tight voice, "and I felt like I was in a fog doing what my family wanted me to do. And now I see things clearly. You weren't wrong about him. We both know that."

"I think I will order something after all. Excuse me." Cheryl grabbed her handbag, went to the counter and stared at the overhead board.

She wasn't really a coffee drinker, but she needed to

get away from Esme and come up with a new strategy. But her mind was blank. Right now she could use a drink. Something neat and strong. Very strong.

"Can I help you?" the clerk said, a chirpy looking young woman with a eyebrow piercing.

"No, I'm just looking." She looked behind her to make sure no one was standing in line. "Give me a second."

"Can I make a suggestion?"

"I'd take one about how to convince a woman to take back her fiancée."

The woman frowned. "What?"

"Never mind. I'll have whatever's popular."

The clerk turned to fix her something and Cheryl sighed. She felt as if she were being played, as if Esme knew she'd gotten her hopes up by agreeing to meet her. Esme was a sneaky woman. She couldn't underestimate her. She'd been arrogant hinting that she could persuade her in one day. She wouldn't easily be persuaded to change her mind. Cheryl chewed her lip. She needed more time, but Bryant wouldn't give that to her. She had two days.

Only two days.

Okay, so Esme wanted five good points about Bryant? That shouldn't be too hard. She had to think... One, he was good looking. Two, he paid on time so he was dependable. Three, he uh...dressed well even though his color scheme was on par with the Addams Family. He was clean. And he...he...

"Ma'am?"

She blinked. "Yes?"

"Your coffee is ready."

"Right thanks." She quickly paid then slowly walked back to the table. She needed more time to think but this would have to do. She sat in her seat and looked at Esme who was sipping her iced coffee looking as innocent as a kitten, but she knew the kitten had claws. She glanced at the chocolate biscotti untouched by her elbow.

Esme caught her gaze. "Want one?"

"No, thanks. I can think of three reasons to give him another chance."

Her eyes sharpened with interest. "Really?"

"Yes. He loves you. He loves you and he loves you."

"Maybe."

"Bryant is not the kind of man to ask a woman to marry him he doesn't have strong feelings for."

"He doesn't have strong feelings. He has: Interested, Annoyed, and Calm. That's about it."

"No, he can be angry."

Esme shook her head. "Bryant doesn't get angry."

Cheryl frowned confused that Esme could be so wrong. "Oh, yes he does. I saw it. He's very angry at me right now."

She leaned in intrigued. "How do you know? Did he shout? Curse? Throw something?"

"It was in his eyes. His voice." She shivered. "It was not pretty."

Esme shrugged nonchalant. "I've never seen him angry so I wouldn't know."

"That means something. I hurt him."

"Bryant doesn't get hurt. I told you he has three emotions."

Cheryl pounded the table, causing Esme to jump. "That's where you're wrong." She lowered her voice, she didn't want to frighten her, but she was getting angry at Esme's disregard for Bryant's feelings. She knew he had them. "Losing you hurt him. He wanted to strangle me. If you'd seen his face you'd see how much he loves you. Deeply. He may not have shown that side of himself before but this time he did and if a man like that could lose control of his temper that must mean something." She thought about how he talked about dreams and the flicker of pain in his eyes and the thought of losing them. Pain, Esme must know how much she could hurt him.

"Really?"

"Yes."

Esme thought for a moment and Cheryl held her breath. *Please take him back. Please see how much he loves you. Please, please, please.* But Esme dashed her hopes when she shook her head. "It won't work. I won't change my mind. He's not the man for me and I can't marry him."

Failure wasn't an option. She couldn't fail. But she had, at least for now. Cheryl sat inside her car and stared up at her house. The beautiful house that had once been filled with so many dreams.

And now she was trying to save one. Bryant's.

She had to do something. She couldn't let Bryant leave and prove to her family that she couldn't manage her own life.

Why couldn't she have kept her mouth shut? She couldn't lose Bryant. He rented one of the largest rooms and he was so dependable—a landlord's dream tenant. So he'd ruined the plants but they could be replaced. She had to do something to convince him to stay. She couldn't stay in this house alone (the hermit didn't count since she hardly saw her). Not again. Never again.

Bryant made it feel lived in. Even though she didn't like the man she'd grown used to the sound of him coming in late at night and leaving early morning. The sound of his voice when he talked to the kid, when she came to visit; them playing games and watching movies in the main room.

Sell it, she could hear her family say. She knew that would be the sensible thing. To walk away, to move on, but she couldn't. Her business was here; her life was here. She sighed. She had to make this work. She had to come up with a plan.

She walked into the house hoping she could make it to her bedroom without being noticed.

"How did it go?" a voice called out from the living room.

Cheryl briefly closed her eyes and swore. He was waiting for her. She walked towards the living room then froze in the entry way. He really did resemble Death. He wore a pressed black shirt and black trousers and slowly rose from the couch like a dark shadow. She half expected large black wings to unfurl and spread out behind him.

"Why do you assume I went to see Esme?"

He gestured to his face. "The makeup and the clothes. You don't usually dress like that."

She felt her face grow warm. Was she that obvious? She glanced down at her cream colored blouse and green skirt. He was right. She'd taken extra special care to try to impress Esme.

He met her gaze and offered her a silent question that said "Am I right?" and the look made her inwardly cringe. She'd hoped to come back with better news. But she wouldn't back down from a minor setback. She had to reassure him. It would be too easy for him to find another place.

She steeled herself for battle and walked into the room. "It will take a bit more persuasion."

"You failed," he said in a flat voice.

"She's still thinking about—"

"Miserably."

"If you give her time—"

"I'm leaving." He began to walk past her.

She grabbed his arm.

He stopped. "What have I told you about touching me?"

She quickly jumped back waving her hands. "Sorry, sorry. Bad habit."

He folded his arms. "What do you want?"

To turn back time. To make this awful thing go away. "I can help you."

He walked past her. "No you can't."

"I can help you win her back."

He paused.

Her heart leapt with hope. She had him, she just

needed to reel him in. "I know she feels something for you, she's just confused. But I know what she wants from you."

He slowly turned and lifted a brow. "What she wants from me?"

Cheryl quickly nodded, eager to convince him. "She needs to see you in a new light. I can help you."

"Considering you ruined my chances what makes you think you can easily fix things?"

"I didn't say it would be easy, but she listens to me. Trusts me. I know what she's looking for in a man and I can help state your case. She listened to me once, what's not to say I can't be persuasive again? And if you make a few minor changes what's the harm in that?"

Bryant sighed and hung his head. "I shouldn't be listening to this," he said to no one in particular.

"But you are because you know it's a good idea."

He lifted his head. "I'll give you three months."

"Three months?"

He nodded, his gaze hard. "Think it will take longer?"

Absolutely. "No, no of course not."

He held out his hand. "Then you're on."

She glanced at his hand wary, it seemed to be as thin and tough as the rest of him. "So you...uh...promise that if you reunite with Esme you'll stay."

He nodded.

"Um...great." She took his hand, surprised by the heat of his palm, the strength in his fingers.

Bryant tightened his grip and pulled her close, his voice like acid. "And if you fail, I'll not only leave, I'll make sure that room never gets rented. I don't like getting my hopes up for no reason." He held her gaze. "Still confident you can do this?"

She swallowed, her pulse pounding in her neck. "Yes, Deat—um Bryant."

He released her. "What's your name again?"

"My name?"

"Yes, I've been calling you a few things in my head but nothing I can say out loud."

Fair enough. "It's Cheryl."

He nodded. "This will be interesting, Cheryl. What's your first plan?"

"I'll let you know."

"The clock starts now."

Once he was out of the room, Cheryl fell on the couch and rested her head back. That was close. She'd nearly lost him.

Three months. She had three months to get Esme to take him back. That shouldn't be too hard. You couldn't toss away feelings that easily. Esme was testing him. She wanted to see what he was willing to do for her. She wanted a more passionate man. He was a man of deep emotions. She'd help them come to the surface and win Esme's heart.

CHAPTER TEN

*W*hat was wrong with him? Had he gone mad?

Bryant sat on the side of his bed and held his head in confusion.

What had made him think to work with his landlord to get Esme back? He should have packed up his bags and left. But she'd given him hope and he was holding onto that hope with both hands.

He swore. He'd given her the upper hand when he shouldn't have. He still remembered how she hesitated even shaking his hand. She could grab his arm, but not shake his hand? *You still have grease underneath your nails*, he could hear his father say. He had half a mind to wash his hands. Did both women think they were better than him?

He was so close to having all that he wanted. Esme had said yes, she'd wanted to marry him once. With a little help he could convince her again. That Cheryl

60

woman owed him. He didn't want to leave either. It felt like admitting defeat. Besides, the place suited him. It was far enough away from the city and his job but not isolated.

He jumped to his feet and swore again. Something about Cheryl bugged him. He didn't like her, never had. But she got under his skin the way no one else did. The first time he'd run over her damn bushes had been an accident. He'd been in a hurry and turned too wide backing out of the drive. The way she'd reacted to the damage one would have thought he'd shattered an expensive crystal glass set. He'd apologized and offered to pay but she wouldn't hear of it. Just didn't talk to him.

The second time...

Yes, she was right (although he'd never admit it) the second time had been on purpose. She'd made him angry. She'd made Hannah cry.

He couldn't stand seeing a kid cry. Hannah already had to deal with her parents' divorce, the fact that her mother spent most of her time in bed when she came over to visit. So she'd baked cookies. On her own. Her father didn't have much time for her and hadn't provided all the supervision she needed to make a good batch. So when she came over and offered them to him he'd ignored the fact that they were burnt on the bottom and dry. He'd eaten them with a smile.

But Cheryl.

Cheryl had taken one bite, said they were awful, told Hannah that she should try again and threw the remainder in the trash before she left.

Hannah stood still, speechless.

Then he saw the tears. A slow, steady stream of tears running down her face. His temper snapped. Cheryl had no right treating a child like that. After treating Hannah to ice cream, a trip to the park and a game on his phone, he'd gotten in his car and made sure he smashed every bush he hadn't demolished the first time through. This time when he saw the outrage on Cheryl's face he inwardly cheered.

He should have been prepared for her revenge. A woman like Cheryl always got her revenge. He'd smashed her plants; she'd smashed his future. He gripped his hand into a fist and swore again. That woman was everything he couldn't stand. Bossy, cold, angry and mean.

But she wanted him to stay. He knew it was for no other reason than for the rent money, not because she liked him. Was she greedy too? He'd use that to his advantage. She was arrogant enough to think that she could help him get Esme back, and part of him wanted her to succeed. He wanted Esme back. No matter what.

His cell phone rang and he thought of ignoring it until he saw the number. He sighed and connected.

"We'll be in town next week," his older brother Quentin said, "and would like to treat you and Esme to—"

"The wedding's off."

"Since when?"

Bryant sat on his bed and stared at the ring on his dresser. "She changed her mind." He wished he'd waited a few days before telling his brother about the engagement then he wouldn't have had to tell him about its demise.

"This must the shortest engagement in history."

He ran a hand down his face. "I'm sure there are shorter."

"Few, what happened?"

He didn't want to go into detail. No matter how he told the story it didn't make him look good. "Did you tell Dad?"

"Nope haven't spoken to him."

That was a relief. His dad would get a chuckle out of this. "I'm going to fix it."

"How?"

He walked over to the dresser, opened the box and stared at the ring. "You'll see."

"That means you don't know."

He touched the diamond wondering if he should have gotten something bigger. "I'll get her back."

"Maybe it's a sign."

"What's a sign?"

"This breakup. Maybe you're not meant to be together."

"Yes, we are." He clenched his teeth and snapped the ring box closed. "I thought you liked her."

"Yes, I do. Very much. And I like you too. That doesn't mean you're good for each other."

"You don't think I'm good enough for her?"

Quentin sighed. "I didn't say that."

Bryant opened a drawer and shoved the box inside. It hurt too much to look at it. "You wouldn't be the first."

"Don't put words in my mouth."

He closed the drawer. "We are perfect for each other."

"How come she doesn't think so?"

I don't know! That was what still bothered him. What had he missed? Cheryl said she knew what Esme wanted from him. Why didn't he? But he wouldn't be too proud, he'd be the man she wanted. "It will all work out."

"Just listen—"

"No."

"Come on Bryant."

"No. Got anything else to say?"

Quentin paused then said, "I know a way you can get a full refund on your ring."

He disconnected and tossed the phone on his bed. He wasn't returning the ring. He was getting Esme back.

He left his room and stopped by the door two down from his. It belonged to Gina "Ginnie" Sanchez, Hannah's mother. "Hey, Ginnie I'm going to the store. Do you need anything?"

No reply.

He went back to his room and looked out the window. Her car was in the drive so that meant she was home. He knocked again. "Come on, Ginnie. Just say yes or no."

He waited. Still no reply.

He pressed his ear against the door. He usually heard her moving around. Not that she did much of that or typing on her laptop. Most of the time she stayed in bed. Especially on the weekends. He pulled out his cell phone and sent her a text. No response. He called her. Still nothing. He knocked and tried the door handle. It was locked. "Ginnie?"

Silence.

Something was wrong.

He started for the stairs to go to the first floor, wondering if Cheryl would give him the keys to Ginnie's place, but he stopped. That woman wouldn't care.

He took a deep breath, turned around and broke down the door. He searched the room but it was empty. That's when he heard the shower. He knocked then entered and saw Ginnie lying naked on the floor. He didn't see any blood, which was a relief. He rushed over to her. "Ginnie, can you hear me?"

"Leave me alone."

He tried to lift her to a sitting position. "What happened?" he said in a soft voice. "Did you slip? Are you hurt? Can you get up?"

"What the hell did you do?" Cheryl demanded, rushing into the room. "It sounded like a bomb going off."

He knew he'd damaged the door, but didn't care. "Get me a towel."

She grabbed one from the towel rack and gave it to him. "You could have asked for a key."

He looked down at the face towel she'd handed him. He angrily tossed it back at her. "Give me something bigger. I need to cover her up."

Cheryl blinked as if finally seeing the full picture. "Oh. Right. Sorry." She turned off the shower then headed for the door.

"Where are you going?" he shouted after her as she left the room. He softly swore and grabbed the body towel from the rack nearby and wrapped it around Ginnie. Moments later Cheryl returned with a large beach towel.

"Go and give her some privacy," she said, replacing the towel he'd wrapped around Ginnie with the one she'd brought.

"No," Ginnie said. "He can stay. I want him to."

"What happened? Do you need an ambulance?"

"No. I just want to sleep."

Bryant frantically searched the bathroom. "Did you take anything?"

"No. I just want to lay here and die of pneumonia."

"It doesn't work that way," Cheryl said.

Bryant glared at her.

Cheryl shrugged. "It's the truth."

Ginnie sniffed. "Hannah's better off without me."

Cheryl jumped to her feet and said to Bryant, "Get her to bed and I'll get her something to wear."

He lifted Ginnie in his arms, shocked by how small and fragile she felt. He needed to check on her more often. He carried her to the bed and gently set her down.

Cheryl stood beside him holding a nightgown. "Close your eyes," she told him.

"Why? I already saw her naked."

"That doesn't matter. Turn around. You shouldn't be enjoying this."

"I'm not," he said, turning his back to them. "It's not like a guy gets a hard-on just seeing a naked woman on the ground. I mean if you had been on the floor naked I'd squeeze my eyes shut so tight to prevent having nightmares."

"That's really mature," Cheryl said, her voice heavy with sarcasm. She softened her tone and said to Ginnie, "I'll get you some tea to drink, okay?" She looked at

Bryant and said, "You can turn around now," before she left the room.

He helped Ginnie into bed then sat down on the edge. "What's going on?"

Ginnie's eyes filled with tears. "He's going to marry her." Bryant knew who 'he' was. Her ex. "I didn't think it would get that serious. But today he told me he's thinking of marrying her. Now Hannah will have another mother."

"She'll always have you."

"But she likes her more."

"You don't know that."

"I do. She tells me how they go out to places. I can't afford those places. Look at where I live, in a room. I used to have a house and a family."

"You still have a daughter. You need to be strong for her. We all hit a hard patch in life, but it's how we rally from it that matters. You don't want Hannah to see you fall apart like this."

"No. She's coming the day after tomorrow. Could you watch her?"

He sighed. He liked Hannah but he wondered if he was doing more harm than good. "She comes to see you. Not me."

"I'll see her. I promise. But I don't have the strength. I can't face her yet."

"You'll feel better."

"But if I don't, could you please help me out?"

"Fine, but just for a couple hours then you have to be with her. You're hurting her more than you know."

Her lower lip trembled. "Because I'm a rotten

mother. I should have found a way to make it work. I should have been a better—"

Bryant covered her hand with his. "Things happen. Blaming yourself won't change anything. Go to sleep."

"Want to join me?"

"You know I'm seeing someone."

Ginnie gave him a watery smile. "She doesn't have to know."

"You don't want to do this."

"Yes, I do," she said in a tear soaked voice. "I want to be held in a man's arms. I want to feel attractive again."

Bryant gathered her close and hugged her. "You are attractive and you'll meet someone else." He kissed her on the forehead. "After you're rested I'll take you out for something to eat. Okay?"

She nodded and slid under the covers. "Esme is so lucky. If she ever lets you go, let me know."

He pulled the blanket to her shoulders. "Sleep well."

Bryant left the room and closed the door. The latch was broken, but at least the door remained on its hinges.

"I'll fix it," Cheryl said.

He turned and saw her holding a tray with a sandwich, steaming cup of tea and cut banana slices and strawberries. Maybe the woman did have a heart.

"She won't need that now," he told her.

"Oh. I'll keep it for later. Are you busy?"

He looked at her with suspicion. "Why?"

"I have a few things I want to ask you."

CHAPTER ELEVEN

He could be tender.

She hadn't expected that. She hadn't meant to overhear Ginnie's conversation with Bryant, but once she started, she couldn't stop. His voice was so patient and caring. Why hadn't Esme seen that side of him when Ginnie had? And the other woman clearly had feelings for him. She may be an emotional mess, but she was still an option and he did like her daughter. Why didn't he get over Esme's rejection and turn to a woman who would eagerly have him?

Shawn was right. Love could be messy and she didn't know where to start. It sounded logical when she said she could help Bryant win Esme back but she didn't know how to proceed.

However, overhearing him had given her an idea. If she wanted to help Bryant she had to get to know him a little more. She inwardly shivered at the thought (she'd probably have better success planting a tree underwater) but if she wanted to keep him in the house it was necessary.

But, when she put Ginnie's food in the fridge then met Bryant in the living room and told him about her intentions, he didn't seem to like the idea anymore than she did.

"My hobbies?" he repeated. He sat across from her looking as cuddly as a cobra. She didn't know how Hannah and Ginnie managed to bring out another side to him.

Cheryl nodded, trying her best to sound sincere. "Yes, do you have any?"

"Why?"

She sighed. "I told you. If I'm going to sell you I have to get to know a little more about you. Nothing too intimate of course, but if I could highlight your good traits it might help."

He fell silent then said, "I might as well just move out now."

"You said you'd give me three months."

"That's when I thought you knew what you were doing."

"You're going to have to trust me. Please tell me something about yourself."

"Like what?"

"What you do in your spare time? What's your favorite color? What do you do for a living?"

"I don't have any particular hobbies. I don't have a favorite color."

"It's not black?"

"No, why?"

She looked at his clothes. "Never mind."

"My favorite color changes. And I design toys."

Cheryl blinked. "As a hobby?"

"As a profession," he said spacing out the words.

"Really?"

"You sound surprised."

"I am." She pictured him as something else. When she'd first met him she'd imagined him as a corporate raider, an investigator, or a grave digger. When he'd put down "designer" as his occupation on his rental application, she'd guessed he worked in graphic design or designing websites. "I've never met a toy designer before."

"Hmmm. But of course Esme already knows what I do for a living since I work for her father's company."

"Which company?"

"Scott Designs. You likely have never heard of it."

He was right but she didn't want to admit it. She looked at him. "You design toys?"

"I already said that."

She bit her lip. "Is that why you hang out with that kid?"

"Kid?"

"The girl with the glasses."

"You mean Hannah?"

She nodded. "Yes. Ginnie's daughter."

"We're friends. I test some theories out on her but we're also friends."

Cheryl chewed her lip. "Oh dear."

"What?"

"I may have also implied that you had an unhealthy attachment to her."

"I know," Bryant said grim. "Esme laughed when she told me that one. I like playing. But I'm not a criminal."

"I'm sorry."

"You've said that."

"I know."

"She also needs a friend."

"I guess so with a mother like that."

He folded his arms. "You don't seem to know very much about us."

"Us?"

"Your renters."

"Your lives are none of my business."

"And you don't care."

"Even if I did, it wouldn't make a difference."

Bryant thought for a moment then nodded. "True enough. She's been divorced a year and shares custody."

"I see."

"She's not taking the divorce well. So when Hannah comes over I keep her company."

"You'd think Ginnie would want to spend time with her."

"It's more complicated than that."

"What's complicated? Moping around wanting things to be different is useless. She should be with her kid."

Bryant tilted his head to the side and studied her. "Her name is Hannah."

"What?"

"She's not just a kid. She has a name. She may not be your business, but you should still know her name."

Cheryl nodded in no mood to fight. "Right. What kind of toys do you design?"

"Action figures, scale models."

"Can I see your work?"

He paused. "Why?"

"I'm curious." And to her surprise she truly was. His choice of occupation intrigued her. She always felt a special kinship with people who liked to build things.

He rested his arm along the length of the couch. "You look at it every day."

She frowned. "No, I don't."

Bryant nodded to the curio set in the corner. "Yes, you do." He stood and walked over to it and pointed to a detailed, action figurine called Altran. It had been one of her husband's favorite characters from a little known sci-fi series from the eighties who'd found a new audience in the 21st century and had a cult following. The series had spawned several movies and books and later merchandise for eager fans willing to pay top price to stay connected to the elaborate world.

Cheryl stared at the object amazed. "You designed this?"

He nodded.

"It was one of Martin's favorite pieces. He said the detail was remarkable and the way you were able to get the image of the actor perfect. So many don't."

"Yes, incredible," Bryant said in a bored tone. "You'd think I was a professional or something."

"I was trying to give you a compliment."

"I don't see how this helps me."

Cheryl studied the figure closer. "I almost can't believe you did this. But you don't seem the type to lie."

He tugged on his ear. "What else do you want to know?"

"Is that why you were talking about dreams? You sell dreams to kids?"

"No, I sell kids a way to learn, imagine and explore."

"You could design anything. Why did you choose to design toys?"

"Because I never wanted to grow up."

It was a glib response and she didn't believe him, but she wouldn't argue. "Okay. Have you ever considered—"

"Yes. What was your favorite toy?"

She paused, startled by the change in topic. Her voice cracked. "My favorite toy?"

"Yes. Growing up," he quickly added, hoping to be clear.

"Oh..."

He cleared his throat, surprising her by looking embarrassed. "I guess I should have been more specific, but since I don't design adult toys I thought you would make the connection."

She felt her cheeks burn. "I wasn't thinking that."

"You sounded shocked."

"By the question. I wasn't thinking about..." Her words fell away.

"Of course not," Bryant quickly said to fill the awkward silence. "But I'm all for play and if you had... I'm not one to judge, but I don't want to know."

"Right, nightmares," she said, reminding him of what he'd said in Ginnie's room about seeing her naked.

"Exactly." He returned to his seat. "So what was it?"

"Why should I tell you?"

"Mine was Hot Wheels." He looked at her and waited.

Cheryl sat down and sighed. Since he'd opened up she had to do the same. She thought for a moment then started to smile as a thought from the past came rushing forward. "I liked Roadmax Dump Truck and Bruder Toys Cat Excavator. I had so much fun with those in my backyard." And for a moment she remembered her excitement when her parents bought the two of them for her birthday and how she'd bought a helmet with her pocket money and pretended she was the main foreperson on a construction site.

She remembered how she had kept the toy excavator until her late teens. She'd taken it with her to the university and had it on her dorm room shelf until it got knocked off by her drunk roommate one night. She remembered telling Martin the story and he'd surprised her with a similar one that she still kept in the office. A toy. It was the first memory of Martin that didn't make her want to cry. She shook her head and stared at Bryant. How had he made her do that? She was supposed to be focusing on him. "Enough about me. Have you ever considered wearing a color other than black?"

Bryant nodded.

Cheryl read his expression and sighed resigned. "And let me guess...you haven't considered it since."

He nodded again. "I knew you were smart."

"However, perhaps if Esme saw you in something different she might see another side to you."

He slowly blinked.

"You're not interested."

He folded his arms and blinked again.

She sighed. "At least think about it."

"I doubt appearing in a green shirt will change anything."

"You never know."

"Right and neither will you."

"Can I see your closet?"

"No."

"I can't help you if you won't let me."

He scratched his chin. "I'm not going shopping."

"So you really only have black clothes?"

"It's practical. A good solid color. Gives me less to think about. Everything matches." He stretched his arm out along the back of the couch and looked at the curio. "How long has it been?"

"Since when?"

"Since your husband died."

He was doing it again, taking her out of the present and thrusting her into the past. She didn't want to tell him. She didn't want to speak to him or anyone about Martin but she felt herself responding anyway. "Two years. We built this house together. A friend of his came up with the design and the moment Martin showed me the blueprint I was in love.

"That was how he proposed. He drove me to this plot of land, showed me the blueprint said 'Let's build a house together' and that was it. I knew I'd found the man for me. And he only got to stay in it for a year before..." She inwardly groaned. What was wrong with her? It wasn't like her to ramble on. He'd only asked when Martin had passed not her life story. She'd shared too much. He didn't need to know that. Why had she said anything? He wasn't interested in her life. He was just making conversation so he didn't have to answer her questions. Why did she keep falling for it?

"That explains it."

"Explains what?" she said, remembering Mrs. Kent's words. Was he going to say she was bitter too?

"I may wear black, but you have it around your heart."

Cheryl jerked her head back, offended. "No, I don't."

Bryant pointed to the curio. "You said that Altran was your husband's favorite character. Altran was an empath. He could take people's pain and morph it into something else. That was his power. I bet your husband left that there because that was his wish for you."

His words were too close to the truth. When Martin had gotten sick he'd referenced the character a lot. Saying how much he didn't want to be a burden. That he wished he could be like Altran and take her pain away. She felt tears and blinked them away. Bryant saw too much.

But like Death he would. He would be all-knowing. This humorless, cold man could casually discuss her dead husband as if he were discussing the weather. Why could he be kind to Ginnie and cruel to her? "You don't know anything about him."

He rose to his feet. "I know enough about you and now I know why you look sad." He shrugged and looked around the room. "You guys worked hard. The place isn't bad."

Cheryl sat frozen. She stared up at Bryant's profile as he looked up at the ceiling.

Look sad? He thought she looked sad? She didn't look sad, did she?

Cheryl shifted her gaze away from him and turned to the curio then quickly looked away wishing, for a moment, that Altran could be real and take all her pain away, or better yet that he could bring Martin back. That she could feel his arms around her once again, hear his laughter, the sound of his footsteps. But instead there was silence.

Too much silence.

She didn't want to talk to Bryant but with him she felt less alone. Why did she suddenly feel that? Why did he make her feel at all? She'd gotten used to feeling nothing. Focusing on her work and the house had been enough but then...then he made her think about love.

Because he blamed her for losing it. Even though she hadn't. Esme was a smart woman, although Cheryl still couldn't understand why Esme thought Bryant lacked emotions. It was clear that he didn't. She'd seen his anger, his pain, his frustration, his compassion and briefly, when he'd looked at the toy he'd designed, she'd seen pride.

She never would have imagined that making toys would have given him pleasure. And he made her talk too much. Why had she told him her favorite toy? Why had he asked?

He'd told her he'd liked Hot Wheels, but somehow that felt like a safe answer. She didn't know why he'd gotten into toys in the first place and he refused to answer her question. He didn't like to reveal much about himself. That would make things more difficult but not impossible.

Then she let his words about the house sink in. She surged to her feet. "What do you mean 'not bad?' This house is amazing. Everyone thinks so."

He lifted a brow. "Really?" he said then strolled into the kitchen.

He was just trying to get under her skin and it was working. Her home was her pride. He could doubt that she might not be able to get Esme back, but when it came to her work there was no doubt. In her profession she had complete confidence.

She found him in the kitchen, strolling around the granite counter like a home inspector. "Who's idea was this?" he said, motioning to the designer cabinets and stove.

"Martin's."

"He liked to cook?"

"No, it was for me."

His brows shot up. "You like to cook?"

He didn't have to sound so surprised. "Used to."

"Do you take requests?"

"I said I *used* to cook."

Bryant tapped his chin. "How about coconut rice and grilled snapper?"

"Did you hear what I just said?"

He rested his hip against the counter. "Think you can manage that?"

"I can manage anything."

"I'd like to see you try."

"Fine."

He pulled out his cell phone. "Dinner. Tomorrow at seven?"

"You're on."

"Great." He made a note, put his phone away then headed for the door.

"Wait! What just happened?"

He slowly turned and shrugged looking the picture of innocence. "You offered to cook me dinner."

"You tricked me."

"Scared you can't do it?"

Yes, she nearly said, but her competitive spirit took hold. "No I—"

"Perfect." He pointed at her. "Make it eight. I'll provide the wine."

CHAPTER TWELVE

You're such a sucker, Bryant chided himself as he made his way to his bedroom.

He didn't even like the woman and now he'd planned to have dinner with her. He'd have to sit across a table from a woman he could barely stand and try to swallow food without choking. He stopped by Ginnie's room and peeked inside. She was soundly sleeping to his relief.

He returned to his bedroom and turned on the TV to see what movies he had in his queue. He'd gotten caught.

It was listening to Cheryl's damn story about her husband and this house. For a moment she was human. Vulnerable and he cared. Damnit. He didn't want to, but he had. Did. She probably didn't even realize how haunted her eyes looked when she talked about the blueprints for the house and how she and her husband had built it together. But he also sensed that she needed to talk about him, that she needed someone to tell.

But after he listened to her, he'd felt guilty for prying, shocked and a little honored that she'd revealed so much about herself that he'd wanted to make her think of something else. Even worse, he'd wanted to give her a hug. He'd actually wanted to touch the woman and tell her that everything would be okay. *What was wrong with him?* She was the last woman who needed his help or would want it.

She'd ruined his life because she hated him so much, why should he care? But her story had him looking at the house in a new way. The main living room probably would have had toys tucked in the corner by now, the fireplace would have been used for the two winters that had passed. The story behind the kitchen had surprised him. The sleek, gourmet design had always impressed him but then to discover that she liked to cook was interesting.

He couldn't help but offer up a challenge.

A challenge that lit her pretty brown eyes and wiped any sadness away.

Pretty? Did he just say her eyes were pretty? He swore and flipped through his movie options. He actually noticed she had pretty eyes...

And she wasn't bad looking if he was honest. His first impression of her was that she reminded him of a Lego brick. Square, solid. When she told him her favorite toy he added a yellow helmet and work boots. It was a cute little image. But then she spoke about her husband and the Lego image fell away and a woman emerged. A woman with a square chin and wide soft mouth. A full, sweet mouth. And hazelnut skin and...

He groaned. It was the artist in him. He couldn't help

noticing details like that. It didn't change anything. He wasn't attracted to her. Hell no... No way. He felt sorry for her. Her loss explained her abrasive personality but didn't excuse it. She owed him and he had to depend on her to help him get Esme back.

He'd eat her cooking and then get back on track. He'd suffer through whatever she made (he doubted it would be very amazing considering she hadn't cooked in awhile) because he had a soft heart, but that would be the end of it.

Bryant nodded then settled on a movie that featured a lot of buildings getting blown up.

"What's his name again?" Cheryl's sister, Maddy, asked her as they stood in the kitchen and unloaded their shopping bags from a recent trip to the grocery store. She was a taller, less stocky version of Cheryl with a chic pixie cut and soft cheeks.

"Bryant Hill. He's a tenant."

"And you're cooking him dinner because..." She let her words trail off for Cheryl to fill in.

"He tricked me." She was still annoyed by how easily she'd been conned, but it got her blood running and her mind thinking. She could manage this. She was still nervous. She hadn't cooked anything complicated in so long, what if she'd lost her touch? Martin had been the only man she'd ever wanted to cook for.

"And how exactly did he do that?"

"He challenged me to cook him something."

"Horrible man," Maddy said with a smile.

"It's not funny. That's why you're here. I'll pay you to do it for me."

"You said you needed help."

"I do," Cheryl insisted. "I need you to help me cook this."

"You can do this yourself."

"I'll pay you."

Maddy shook her head. "No."

"Please. He won't know the difference."

"Yes, he will," a male voice said from the doorway.

he two sisters turned.

"What are you doing here?" Cheryl asked.

He walked up to Maddy. "I'm Bryant."

"Maddy," her sister said with a grin. "And don't worry, I wasn't planning on doing anything. Cheryl is a great cook."

"She doesn't seem to think so."

"I just don't want to cook for you," Cheryl said.

He shoved his hands in his pockets. "You could have said no."

"That's impossible for her," Maddy said. "Did you tell him about our Easy Bake battles?"

Cheryl sent her sister a look. "Why would I tell him that?"

"What's an Easy Bake battle?" Bryant asked.

"It's a competition we used to have with our Easy Bake Ovens," Maddy said. "Our parents would be judges and we'd come up with different desserts."

"Maddy won most of the time," Cheryl added. "But when I won I won big."

"She's right. You should have seen the six-layer, multicolored cake she once made. Mom has a picture of it somewhere."

"I had to beat you at something since you're great at everything else."

"That's not true."

"Says the favorite child."

Maddy shrugged knowing there was nothing to say. They both knew the truth. "I'm still not perfect."

"If you're not going to help you might as well leave." She nodded towards the door.

"Don't you want me to help you put things away?"

"No." She looked at Bryant. "You too. I like to work alone."

He waved his finger at her. "I will, but don't try to order takeaway. I'll find the cartons."

"This dinner is going to make you drool."

"We'll see."

Once they were gone, Cheryl rested her palms on the cold granite counter and tried to calm her heart. She was terrified. For the past couple years the most she'd managed was heating up a pizza in the oven. The rest went straight into the microwave. What if she failed? What if she couldn't do this? It hurt too much to remember that she'd once been the happiest in this room. That she'd eagerly entered it wondering what new recipe she'd surprise Martin with. She liked the chemistry and construction of cooking and Martin always enjoyed whatever she made for him. Even when it was a failure.

Especially when it was a failure. They'd laugh and he'd tease her for days afterwards.

If she failed with Bryant he wouldn't tease her, he'd taunt her—mercilessly. She couldn't let that happen. She closed her eyes and took a deep breath then opened her eyes and began to gather the ingredients. She didn't know how much time passed before she heard a deep voice say, "Something smells amazing."

Her heart leapt and for a moment she was sucked into the past. She half expected Martin to come up behind her, wrap his arms around her waist, and feel the tender brush of his beard as it swept against her cheek and he leaned forward, over her shoulder, to see what she was cooking. And he'd smell like wood and steel. She'd turn to him and see his smiling face...

"You might have me drooling after all," Bryant said.

His words brought her quickly back into the present. Martin wouldn't say something like that or sound so ironic.

She took a deep breath. She'd serve the food then it would be over.

Bryant came up behind her and she froze. She didn't want to move back and touch him. She didn't want her body to remember the feel of a man's touch. She didn't want to touch any man, feel his warm chest pressed against her back, especially this man.

"Move back," she told him.

He leaned over her shoulder and sniffed the air. "Hmm. That really smells good."

He didn't touch her but he was close. Too close. Close enough that for a moment she smelled a faint, sweet raspberry scent. Why did he smell like raspberries? He made her think of lollipops and rollercoaster rides. "Bryant."

"What?"

"I said move back, I have to open the oven and check the fish."

He eagerly grabbed two oven mittens and pushed her aside. "I'll do it." He checked inside. "Looks great. Another couple minutes."

She looked at him surprised. He really looked...not happy but excited if that were possible. She must be imagining it. No man would care that much about a stranger cooking for them. No doubt Esme's meals were fifty times more elegant. Or better yet, her chef's meals. "Did you think I'd burn it?" Cheryl said in a dry voice.

Bryant gently closed the oven and replaced the oven mitts. "I wouldn't put anything past you," he said then softened his words with a grin.

She didn't want to like his grin, but she did. It was sweet and unexpected, like a surprise toy in a box. She could understand why Esme found him hard to read. She knew he didn't like her very much so what was he grinning for? And why did her traitorous heart seem to respond?

She didn't care. She turned away from him and said in a brusque voice, "Sit down."

Bryant walked up to the table. "Wow," he said impressed. "You even set the table."

Yes, she'd brought out her best china and wine glasses and cloth napkins. *Presentation is everything,* her mother had taught her. Even if the food wasn't top notch the eyes, not just the tongue, were part of the equation. "Did you expect paper plates?"

"I didn't know what to expect," Bryant said, taking a seat. He set a bag on the table. "I brought the wine as promised."

The bag completely ruined the décor. "At least take it out of the bag. What are you, a hobo?"

A quick expression of hurt and embarrassment touched his eyes then disappeared. He took the bottle out of the bag and set it on the table. "Sorry."

She inwardly kicked herself. Did she have to sound so mean? She picked up the bottle. "No, I am. I get snippy when I'm nervous." She read the label and kissed it. "This is marvelous. I'll get you the opener."

"I know where it is."

Of course he did. He lived here. "Right. Let me get the food." She placed the coconut rice and red snapper on the table. She watched him fill his plate then take a bite. She held her breath. She didn't want to. She didn't want to care. She knew the dinner would be good—not great, not amazing—just good. If he didn't like it that was not her fault, he had bad taste. But her heart still hammered as she waited for a verdict.

For a moment she was seven-years-old again standing next to her Easy Bake Oven waiting for her mother to tell her if she'd beaten her sister or not.

She lifted her wine glass, pleased her hand wasn't shaking.

Bryant set his fork down and folded his arms. "I won't eat another bite."

She nearly choked on her wine, her heart fell. "You don't like it?"

He stared down at the plate for a long moment then met her eyes. "I won't eat another bite unless you promise me you'll stop committing a crime."

"A crime?" *He hated her cooking that much?*

"Yes, a crime. Letting a skill like this go to waste is criminal." His face spread into a wide grin. "This is delicious."

She gripped her wine glass, part of her wanting to throw the contents in his face for tricking her and the other part wanting to hug him.

It was that grin.

That sneaky, semi-sexy grin.

What was it about his grins that made her feel warm all over? Why did it make her notice the light in his brown eyes, the soft curve of his bottom lip?

"Go on," he said. "Promise me."

Promise me, Martin had begged her. Promise me you'll keep doing what you love. Why was this man asking her to do the same?

She set her glass down. "Why?"

"Because you're not doing this kitchen any favors by not using it."

"I don't have a reason to cook."

"Even for yourself?"

"No."

"Friends?"

She nodded to his plate. "Eat before the food gets cold."

"You have to promise me first."

She sighed. Cooking hadn't been as stressful as she'd thought it would be, and it had been fun to return to it. It had taken her mind off things. She might not love it as she'd once had but she could see herself cooking another meal for when Maddy came over or even for Shawn. "Okay, I promise."

Bryant nodded pleased and picked up his fork. "Great. Can I make another request?"

She scooped up her rice. "No."

"Brownies?"

"No."

"With chocolate frosting."

Cheryl narrowed her eyes. "I'm not making something else for you."

Bryant shook his head. "No, forget the chocolate frosting make it black and white."

"You're not listening to me."

"And if you want to add peppermint shavings I'm open to it."

Cheryl rolled her eyes. "And sprinkles too?"

"Definitely."

She couldn't help a laugh. "You *are* a big kid."

"Guilty. This is so good you could almost convince me to stay just for the food alone." He pointed his fork at her. "Notice I said 'almost' you're not off the hook."

Cheryl smiled at his playful warning, she never thought he could be playful. How come she'd never seen this side of him before? *If Esme ever lets you go, let me know,* Ginnie had said and for a wild moment she could understand why. Bryant had his moments.

Esme must have seen them and if she hadn't Cheryl

would help her to. And his words gave her an idea. She could sweeten the deal a little. If he really liked her cooking perhaps if things with Esme took longer to resolve than three months, she could lengthen the time with some sweet persuasion.

Martin hadn't liked sweets very much. She usually ended up baking things and finishing them on her own or handing them out at work. She glanced at Bryant. She wouldn't have thought he liked sweets either. He looked like a black coffee, banana and plain yogurt kind of guy. The wine he'd chosen for the meal was perfect. The right complement. Sensual in body and taste.

But sensual wasn't cutting it with Esme. Not yet, she would have to come up with a solid plan to convince Esme to give Bryant a second chance.

CHAPTER FOURTEEN

The kid didn't like her.

Cheryl caught Hannah sending her a cutting look as Cheryl walked past the main room where Hannah and Bryant played a video game together.

She didn't know why the kid didn't like her. She'd barely interacted with her, but Hannah made it clear she wanted Cheryl to keep her distance. That didn't bother her, she was used to being disliked. She'd been on an all male crew for a lot of jobs; she'd been one of four females in her engineering class. She'd dealt with animosity.

She could deal with an eight-year-old girl, even though she wondered where the kid's dislike came from. She finally got a hint when Hannah approached her in the kitchen as Cheryl was grabbing a bottle of juice from the fridge.

"Can I ask you something?" she said.

Cheryl closed the fridge and turned to the girl. It was the first time she'd paid attention to her and looked at her up close. Hannah was as daintily built as her mother, dark-skinned like her father and wore her long, black hair pulled back in two large braids.

Cheryl lifted a shoulder in a semi-shrug. "Sure."

"Are you seeing Bryant?" she asked.

Cheryl started to laugh.

Hannah frowned and angrily pushed her glasses up on her nose.

Cheryl covered her mouth to stop her laughter. She waved her hand, not wanting to give the kid another reason to dislike her anymore than she did. "I'm sorry. I'm not laughing at you. It's the question. No, I'm not seeing him."

"But you had dinner with him. He told me."

And why would he do that? But that wasn't her business. "Yes, as a challenge. A bet," she clarified. "He's with someone else." Or hopefully soon will be.

Hannah released a heavy sigh. "I know. Esme."

"So you can talk to her instead of me."

She folded her arms. "I don't like you."

Cheryl opened her juice bottle. "I know."

"Don't you want to know why?"

She took a long swallow then replaced the cap and said, "Not really. You wouldn't be the first and I doubt you'll be the last."

Hannah's arms fell to her side. She stared at her confused. "You don't care?"

"That you don't like me?"

She nodded.

Cheryl shrugged. "Should I? Are we friends?"

Hannah shook her head.

"Do you plan to be my friend?"

She shook her head again.

"Then there's your answer. Is there anything else?"

She shook her head a third time."

"Good," Cheryl said then left the kitchen to get some work done in her office. The kid may not like her, but she certainly was amusing.

"What's up?" Bryant asked, coming into the kitchen. When Hannah hadn't returned to the main room he'd started to worry about her. "I thought you wanted to get something to drink."

Hannah rested her hands on her hips. "Your landlady is strange."

"Landlord," he corrected her. "Trust me you don't want her to hear you call her anything else."

Hannah furrowed her brows perplexed. "Really strange."

"You only just noticed that?" He opened a cupboard and pulled down a cup.

"She doesn't care how I feel."

Bryant turned sharply to her. "What did she say? Did she hurt your feelings?"

"No, she doesn't care that I don't like her."

He opened the fridge and pulled out a jug of apple juice. "Join the club."

Hannah's face brightened. "You don't like her either?"

He poured the juice in the glass, amused by the expression on her face. "Not really."

"Oh good."

He handed her the cup. "That makes you happy?"

She finished the juice in one long swallow then set the cup on the counter, wiping her mouth with the back of her hand. "Yes," she said, taking his hand. But before he could ask why she said, "Come on. Let's go back. I was winning."

Cheryl stood back and looked at her handiwork pleased with herself. She'd finally gotten a chance to fix Ginnie's door. She slid her hand around the doorframe and looked at the lock. Nobody would be able to tell any damage had been done.

She glanced down when her cell phone alerted her to a text. She smiled at the picture of an empty plate and note of thanks Ginnie had sent her. She'd prepared the woman a light mandarin and walnut salad. A hermit had to eat and she was glad to help. Maybe, in time, the food would help her to gain the strength to get over her ex-husband and spend more time with her daughter.

Cheryl put her phone away then gathered her tools and returned them to her tool kit.

"Hannah and I were talking about you," Bryant said.

Cheryl closed the kit and stood. "I always wondered what you two talked about. Don't you have better things to do?" She headed for the stairs. Annoyed that she was a little cheered that he'd been talking about her. Why should it matter?

"She told me she doesn't like you."

"And you told her you don't like me either and you both had a fun giggle, right?"

"No, I was surprised."

Cheryl walked outside then turned into the garage and placed her toolkit inside. "Why?"

"She usually likes everybody. Do you know why she doesn't like you?"

She sent him a look of pity. "Of course I do. I thought you were smarter than that."

"Smarter?"

"Can't you tell when a kid has a crush on you?"

His brows shot up. "A crush? On me? No way. It's the cookies."

"What cookies?"

"She baked us cookies. You said they were awful."

Cheryl searched her mind but came up blank. "Were they?"

Bryant hung his head. "That's not the point." He glared at her. "You were too cruel. You didn't think about her feelings."

"You want to talk about feelings when you have a girl mooning over you with a crush the size of the sun?"

"Hannah does not have a crush on me. Besides, she's too young."

Cheryl rolled her eyes and headed back inside. "No, she's not. So be careful."

"That's not it. I'd...sense something if that was true. She doesn't like you because—"

Cheryl stopped in the foyer and turned to him. "She doesn't want me too close to you. You should see the daggers in her eyes when she looks at me."

Bryant closed the door behind him. "I can sympathize."

"That's my first proof," Cheryl said ignoring the insult. "Secondly, she sighed with sadness when I mentioned Esme. Thirdly, she was upset when you told her about our dinner. Why did you do that anyway?"

"Because I liked your cooking, it wasn't personal."

"She didn't know that. It really bothered her. That's a sign."

Bryant shook his head. "And I think you're wrong. She knows we're buddies."

The man was clueless. Both mother and daughter had feelings for him and he didn't see it. "For her sake, I hope you're right."

CHAPTER FIFTEEN

He knew the smell of failure.

It smelled like glue and melting plastic. Bryant looked at the startled, horrified face of Marie Yoh who'd only been with Scott Designs for a year. She opened her mouth and he knew he'd hear the beginning of an apology so he shook his head to stop her. "It's okay. Better that happened to you than a child. Find out what went wrong and fix it." She nodded relieved and began to clear up her work.

He didn't know why she needed to look so relieved. He rarely got angry. He'd made Scott Designs a place for experimentation. He expected things to go wrong. When he'd first come on board the company had suffered a major financial hit when another designer had rushed an idea to market based on an expensive prototype that hadn't been thoroughly tested. Esme had been one of the major supporters of the project. The toy died in the marketplace for a number of reasons one being a major piece breaking off after use.

After that, Marlon became stringent with his budget and gun shy about paying for prototypes unless they were using someone else's investment. He wanted guaranteed hits that ultimately strangled the creativity of the designers who hadn't left for better opportunities and led to nearly two years of flops. Bryant was able to assess the problem and do some maneuvering to rebuild Esme's confidence in herself and her judgment, renew Marlon's faith in the business and reignite happiness in the employees by orchestrating a lucrative licensing deal that put the company back in the black and created a steady stream of revenue that grew year after year.

But new designers were still hesitant when they did fail, curious to see if he stood by his word that it was a safe environment to try new things. He was pleased that he was able to keep his promise.

Bryant went into his office and stopped when he saw Cheryl. He paused, surprised by how happy he was to see her. It had been about a month since their first meal together and they'd made it a habit of having her prepare something every Friday. She told him it was a way for her to get to know him better. He convinced himself he did it for the meals.

When he'd asked her to make him coconut rice and red snapper he'd done so because he pitied her and he'd had every intention of hating every bite.

But then he was slowly seduced by the scent of lemons, paprika and ginger. He peeked inside the kitchen and watched her and as he watched her unnoticed, he learned a lot more about her. She definitely had the mind of an engineer. Everything was methodical and organized, well paced and carefully executed focusing on the end design. He smiled to himself when he watched her make a mix, taste it with the tip of her pinkie then toss it away in disgust before she started over.

She really wanted to win. She wanted to show him she could cook and for a moment he could picture her as a little girl competing against her sister, the focused gaze and set jaw. When he knew the meal was almost ready he'd come in ready to get the challenge over with. Then he saw the table.

He hadn't noticed when she'd set it so she must have done it before she'd started cooking. The table was what truly shocked him. Nobody had ever set a table like that for him before. The gray cloth napkins had been shaped into a fan, the white plates had a gleaming silver trim. He'd been so surprised he'd briefly forgotten his manners and set his bag on the table. She'd quickly corrected him, making him feel like a grease hog who'd come in tracking car oil through the kitchen.

And he remembered who he was with and why he didn't like her and he was determined not to like her food either.

But then the damn woman kissed the bottle, told him it was marvelous then served him a meal he'd never forget.

Ever. The rice was light and flavorful, the fish, firm and flaky. It didn't fall apart. And he learned something else about her that evening. She was hiding.

She was hiding from passion and pleasure. Wasting

her skills because her husband was gone. He didn't know much about grief, but he could imagine that closing off this side of her had made her mean. She needed to cook. Cooking was good for her and if he benefited from her desire to get to know him better that was even better.

He didn't want to like her, he still didn't like her, but he didn't dislike her as much as before. He'd started to understand her more and she'd become more tolerable (she'd even treated him and Ginnie to a sautéed scallop dish that had his mouth watering in memory). But she'd never visited his office before and he wondered if she'd come to deliver bad news. Was she cancelling their next dinner? He'd been looking forward to it. But then he looked at her face and sighed. He knew that expression—she looked earnest and eager—and that meant she wanted him to do something.

"What's up?"

"I didn't realize you dressed up for work."

He glanced down at his suit. She was right. He usually wore black jeans and a shirt, but today he wore a black fitted jacket and trousers. "I'm meeting with a representative later. I have to sell them an idea. It helps to look professional."

"I see." She held out a square, glass container. "Here."

"What's this?"

"The brownies you requested. I—"

He stopped listening. She'd finally made them. He wasn't sure she ever would and now they were here. He eagerly lifted the lid and inhaled the scent. "You could have waited until I got home."

"I know, but then I realized this could be part of our plan."

He took a brownie and bit into it. "Damn, this is so good. What did you do to make it so soft?"

"It's a secret. Now focus. You need to—"

"I've never tasted this kind of icing before."

"This is what I want you to do. Are you listening?"

Bryant licked chocolate off his thumb and made a noncommittal sound.

Cheryl watched his pink tongue make the sweet, soft crumb disappear and swallowed. She'd been trying to seduce him with food for the past several weeks to distract him from the fact that her plan was failing. She'd encouraged him to ignore Esme, that hadn't worked. She'd instructed him to invite her for coffee to show he had no hard feelings, she'd turned him down. A funny (to show Bryant's sense of humor) animation sent to her cell phone had gotten them nowhere.

Month two was here and if she didn't do something drastic Esme would be snapped up by another man and Bryant would never forgive her. Fortunately, he was too busy enjoying her cooking to realize she was getting a little desperate.

Partially because she was starting to like their little ritual. She was starting to like him. Too much. He was fun to cook for and complain to. When she had a bad day he took her griping in stride. If she wasn't careful she might actually end up liking him and that was something she never wanted to do. She didn't mind being cordial and polite, but liking him? Caring about him? Missing him when he wasn't home? Wondering what he was up to when he was? That was out of the question. Besides, he had no interest in her whatsoever. Nor she in him.

Even though, sometimes, she found herself watching him. Like now as he licked his bottom lip, briefly closed his eyes, making a low groan of pleasure. And she wanted to make him groan more, except he wasn't eating a brownie he was eating her. Slowly.

Cheryl shook her head. Whoa! Where had that thought come from? Her only goal was to help him get Esme back. Today she had a new strategy that had to work and she needed him to focus.

"Bryant, what I'm going to say next is important. Go to Esme and share the brownies with her."

He shook his head.

"Why not?"

"She's not into chocolate."

"Seriously?"

He nodded.

"Why didn't you say so? I've been grilling you for all this time and you're just telling me this now?"

"I didn't think it was important."

"You asked for brownies."

"For me, not for her. It was a personal request."

Cheryl sighed and muttered to herself. "I was sure at the coffee shop that she had chocolate covered biscotti."

"She orders them for her mother."

"What does she like then? Carrot cake? Angel cake? A strawberry tart?"

"She doesn't like baked goods. She prefers to stick with fruits."

"Do you think she'd liked grilled peaches and pineapple? Or baked banana?"

His face split into a wide grin. "I would."

She frowned. "I'm not talking about you."

He shrugged. "I don't know. But could I make a request for that too?" He took another bite then held out the container to her.

Cheryl shook her head. "It's all yours."

"Go on. It's not bad."

She laughed. "High praise indeed."

"I've really never tasted a brownie like this."

"It's probably the spinach."

He met her eyes. "Really?"

"Yes."

"Even better. I can have this for dinner instead of vegetables."

"Don't get carried away." She took a step back. It was time to go home and regroup. She couldn't stay even though a part of her wanted to. She liked seeing him in his suit, he looked fierce and professional and sexy. She took another hasty step back. It was probably the scent of chocolate that was messing with her mind. He wasn't sexy, he was just Bryant. She definitely needed to get out of there. "I'll talk to you later."

He glanced up, shifted his gaze past her and looked at something through his office window. "Wait. Don't leave yet."

"Why not?"

"Esme just came out of her office. Keep talking to me until she goes back in."

"Why?"

"Because I want her to see you talking to me."

"Again...why?"

His dark gaze met hers. "Just do it."

"Fine, I'm talking to you. Talk. Talk. Talk." Cheryl opened and closed one hand as if it were a puppet. "And more talk. Talk. Talk. Will that do?" she asked, then paused as she watched a sly grin spread over his lips.

"Yes," he said, glancing past her. "I think it will. Your plan might work after all."

That grin. Why did that grin always make her heart pick up pace? She tugged on her collar wondering why she suddenly felt so warm. "My plan? You're going to give her a brownie? You're going to tell her about the spinach?"

Bryant shook his head. "No, I think Esme seeing me with you is making her think twice. She looks interested." His gaze met and held hers. "And you're the key."

"I'm the key?"

He nodded. "I've come up with a plan of my own. And I think it might work. We'll talk after I get off work." He bent down and kissed her on the mouth. "Don't get mad. I'll explain that later," he whispered against her lips before he straightened. "She's still looking at us."

Cheryl stood stunned and almost said "Who?" before she caught herself. He'd kissed her! Bryant had kissed her. On the mouth. What had happened? Her lips still tingled from the touch of his. He tasted like chocolate and peppermint icing. And the worst part was that she felt far from angry at him.

Bryant walked to the door and opened it then said, "Thanks for the brownie. I'll see you at home." He kissed her on the lips again. "I promise I'll explain everything tonight."

CHAPTER SIXTEEN

Cheryl stared at Bryant as if he'd started levitating. He couldn't be suggesting what she thought he was. But that wasn't what left her speechless. It was him sitting beside her in the family room and showing her his idea in storyboard form on his tablet. She didn't know when he'd had the time to come up with the plan, but the story looked intriguing. He even got all their features right. Except for the fact that Esme looked like the queen, Bryant the noble knight and Cheryl the helpful sidekick—his kitchen maid.

"A girl's dream," she mumbled.

"What?"

"Never mind." She shifted away from him too aware of how his thigh pressed against hers. "You want us to pretend to be a couple?"

He shifted, closing the gap between them as he pointed to a panel on the screen. "Yes."

"Why?"

He frowned. "I just showed you."

She nodded to the pictures and shifted again. "You just showed me a nice fairy tale."

He scooted over, his voice firm. "It can work."

Cheryl sighed as his thigh once again brushed against hers. If she scooted further she'd be trapped between the arm of the couch and him.

"Because for the first time Esme looked at me in a way she hasn't before. She looked really interested." He leaned closer and pointed to a panel that showed the noble knight and his kitchen maid in an embrace with the queen watching with envy.

Cheryl pressed her hands together in her lap imagining that moment being real. Except she wasn't a lowly kitchen maid. She was a high member of the court who had built the castle in which the queen lived. A castle so magnificent it had gained attention from faraway kingdoms and he was one of the princes so impressed with her skill he'd traveled days to find her and ask her to run off with him and...

"That's a ridiculous story," she muttered.

"You don't like it?"

She swore. Did she say that out loud? "Uh...No it's not that." She drummed her fingers on the armrest. He didn't like to be touched, but right now she had a wild urge to press her hand against his chest and push him away. Or pull him closer which was much worse. She gripped one hand into a fist. He wasn't her type. He was too lean. She liked her men big, more muscular, but if that were true why did her gaze keep dipping to how Bryant's black shirt spread across his chest?

It was the stupid kiss. The kiss had confused her.

"I've thought this through," Bryant said.

Cheryl jumped to her feet no longer able to sit so near to him. She folded her arms and faced him. "She dated you for two years I'm sure she was interested."

"But not like this. It's pure psychology. Your interest in me makes her see me in a new way."

She silently swore. He was on to something. She hated to admit it, but it was a solid plan. She wished she'd thought of it sooner. She'd wasted a month. She'd let herself become too attached to him. Of course pretending to be his girlfriend wouldn't make that any easier. But if Esme really got jealous she could have them reunited within the week. Bryant would go back to his regular life and she'd keep him as a tenant and everyone's problems would be solved.

She nodded. "Okay, I agree. I could pretend that I said those things about you so that she would move herself out of the picture so that I could swoop in and take you."

He frowned. "You make me sound like prey."

"It's primal. Her jealousy proves she still has feelings for you."

"We don't know if she's jealous yet."

"We'll make her jealous and then use it to our advantage."

He nodded, looking relieved. "Exactly."

"So do you want me to bake you another batch of brownies and deliver it?"

He leaned back, grinning like a kid. "Absolutely and then we'll start the plan."

Her arms fell to her side. "That *was* part of the plan."

"No, you delivering food isn't enough. We need to make this more public. I have a party coming up. You'll be my date."

"That might not be a good idea. I'm not good at parties."

"Just say nice things about me this time and you'll be fine. If this all goes well you might be off the hook sooner than you think."

Cheryl rubbed her hands on her jeans, wishing his words gave her more reassurance. "What should I wear?"

He scratched the back of his head. "Clothes would be nice."

"If it's fancy, I'm not interested. I can't afford fancy."

"It's business casual."

"What does that mean?"

He paused. "It means 'business casual'."

"Look, unless you want me to show up in a pantsuit you need to be more specific."

He looked her up and down. "Do you own a dress?"

She was on the verge of a meltdown. Cheryl stared at her closet in dismay. She hadn't gone to anything in years. Even when she was with Martin they hardly went to fancy events. *Don't panic. Don't panic. Don't panic.* She needed reinforcement.

Her sister stared at the closet and shook her head. "I'm glad you called me."

"Is there anything I can do?" Cheryl said hopeful.

"Buy a dress."

"I don't want to go shopping."

Maddy held up an outdated flower patterned dress. "You cannot help him win his girlfriend back wearing this. We're going shopping."

"I didn't budget this."

"Do you want to keep your tenant or not?"

She was right. If everything went according to plan this charade could all be over within a week.

Two days later Cheryl stood looking at her reflection hardly recognizing herself. Her sister had helped her with her makeup and pulled her hair up in a twist. She hadn't done anything with her hair in so long it was a surprise to see how much the new style changed her face. It was also a little terrifying. She didn't like drawing attention to herself like this. She wasn't in the same league as Esme, a woman used to turning heads just by breathing, but it was for a good cause. One pretend date, perhaps by the end of the evening a jealous Esme would call Bryant up and beg him to take her back.

Her cell phone rang. It was Shawn.

"Where are you?" he demanded once she picked up.

"What do you mean?"

"I needed you to sign off on a major purchase."

She swore. She'd forgotten she'd promised to meet him in the office for the two signature verification that would allow him to buy new equipment he needed. "I'll be right there."

She hurried down the hall and walked into the office. "I'm so sorry," she said, grabbing a pen. "I hope I didn't keep you waiting long." She looked on her desk. "Where's the form?"

He stared at her.

"Shawn? Where's the form?"

He looked flustered. "Um...yea right the form." He took it from his desk and placed it in front of her."

She signed it. "Now you're all set. I hope this makes the job easier."

He nodded. "Right. Yes, they said it'd be fine."

"Who?"

"You said they were good clients."

"I said no such thing. I said I hope this makes the job easier."

He rubbed his forehead and nodded again. "Right."

She frowned. "Are you okay? Do you think you're coming down with something?"

He shook his head and gestured to her amazed. "I just haven't seen you look like this in a while. Maybe ever."

Cheryl looked down then realized what had startled him. Damn, she'd forgotten about the clothes, the makeup and the hair.

"It's business related," she said with a dismissive wave of her hand.

His gaze trailed down her dress. "What kind of business?"

"Get your mind out of the gutter."

A smile danced around his lips. "What are you up to? Can I play too?"

"No. This is part of my strategy to help Bryant win Esme back."

"By seducing him?"

"What are you talking about?" Cheryl said with a laugh. "This outfit is to make Esme jealous."

Shawn pulled on his beard uncertain. "I'm not sure he'll even notice Esme tonight. I wouldn't."

"You're embarrassing me."

"You have no idea how beautiful you look right now."

She smiled. He'd given her the confidence she needed. "You're the sweetest brother-in-law in the world."

He shook his head. "I'm serious. You look...amazing."

"I'm doing this once. And then I'll turn back into a hammer."

"I think you mean a pumpkin."

"It's my fairy tale I want to be more useful," she put her pen away.

"Actually, I don't think Cinderella turns into a pumpkin. I mean that would be cool, but I don't think that's how the story goes."

She playfully tugged on his beard. "My point is that this fiasco is only for one night."

He covered her hand, his face pensive. "It shouldn't be. Martin wouldn't want that for you."

She looked away, she didn't want to talk about Martin tonight. "I'd better go before I'm late."

She hurried down the hall and saw Bryant's back as he waited in the family room. "I'm sorry. Jeez, that's all I seem to be saying today. But I had to do some work before I finished getting ready."

Bryant spun around and paused. He didn't look shocked and flustered like Shawn. But he had an expression on his face that she'd never seen before. There was a quiet, hungry intensity in his gaze that made her go hot.

Was he scrutinizing her? Wondering if she made a worthy adversary for Esme? "Am I overdressed?"

He shook his head.

"Underdressed?"

He shook his head again.

She smiled. "Just right?"

He shook his head.

Her smile fell and her confidence dipped a little. "What's wrong?"

"Nothing," he said in a gruff voice. "Finish getting ready. I'll meet you in the car."

ryant remembered the first time he'd fallen in love. He'd been eight-years-old and the object of his affection had been a fire engine red Hot Wheels car with a splash of yellow on the side. He hadn't had much growing up and had redesigned the Hot Wheels track to suit him in order to make the car go as fast and high as it could. For one wild moment as he stared at Cheryl in her red dress she turned into that car, his gaze taking in every round curve, every angle. And he wanted to get inside and drive.

Drive her hard.

Drive her fast.

Drive her higher than she ever thought possible. He wanted to make her engine roar.

Bryant stepped out into the cool spring night and took a deep breath as he walked towards his BMW, which was nothing like the red car of his childhood dreams. It was sleek and black. Esme looked good in it and so did he. It fit his image. Professional and sophisticated.

He pulled out his keys and accidentally dropped them on the ground. When he bent to pick them up he noticed his hand was shaking. He swore. He took another deep breath. So Cheryl was pretty. More than pretty. Sexy. Attractive. He'd seen an attractive woman before. He needed to get a hold of himself.

He opened the car door and sat inside, drumming his fingers on the steering wheel. He didn't like Cheryl. Not like that. But he still felt guilty. Esme was supposed to be the only woman he looked at, thought of, wanted.

He looked up and saw Cheryl locking the front door then turn and head towards him. The black shawl draped around her shoulders briefly reminded him of a cape and he pictured her as an action figure who could make a building rise up from the ground fully structured and perfect, with just the casual twist of her hand.

She wasn't elegant. She wasn't refined. She didn't fit his image. There was too much fire there. Too much heat. He briefly closed his eyes.

Why did he feel like he was lusting after another man's wife? Esme was the only woman he wanted.

Cheryl opened the door, slid into the passenger seat and with one glance she turned him into a liar. At that moment he didn't want Esme, he wanted nothing more than to lean in closer to her and inhale the faint sweet scent of papaya that scented her skin. He wanted to unzip her dress and run his hand along...

"Tell me what's wrong," Cheryl demanded.

"W-what?"

"You just swore. Did you forget something? Do you need something?"

Bryant turned on the ignition and mumbled, "A cold shower."

"What?"

He shook his head. He didn't need a cold shower. He needed an ice storm. "Never mind."

"Bryant. Turn off the car."

"Why?" he said, inwardly groaning. She was in one of her bossy moods tonight.

"I want to talk to you."

"You can talk, while I drive."

"We've hardly made it out of the driveway." She covered his hand with hers. "Look at me."

"You're touching me," he said in a low, warning voice.

"I know."

"It's dangerous to do that."

"Then park the car."

He sighed and did. He forced himself to look at her. "Okay."

"I won't let you down," she said removing her hand. "I know this is my fault and I know how bad you want this to work. You don't have to be nervous."

"I'm not nervous."

"I'm going to do whatever it takes to fix this."

"Good," he managed to say, tearing his gaze away from her eyes. They fell to her lips instead.

Her red lips.

Her lush, red lips.

He'd tasted them before. Briefly. He knew they were soft, sweet. But it had been too short. He wanted to know more. Much more.

"You don't believe me," she said in a flat voice.

He swallowed and lifted his gaze. "Believe what?" he said in a low voice that didn't sound like his own.

She was too close. It wouldn't take much to lean closer...

"That I can do this."

He turned away. "I do believe you." He started the car. "Let's go," he said and held up his hand. "And don't touch me again."

"I'll have to touch you a little at the party if we're supposed to pretend to be a couple."

Yes, she was right. That would be a problem because he actually looked forward to the prospect of her touching him. Taking his hand in hers, touching his face, brushing something from his collar. Maybe he *was* nervous. This wasn't like him. Why would he be attracted to someone like Cheryl? They were too different. He didn't like her. She made kids cry, she was still deeply in love with her dead husband, she could be caustic and bossy and she didn't like him. Those were enough reasons to stay away. The only reason she'd dressed up was to make another woman jealous.

Another woman whose name was...Her name was...umm...She was beautiful and he loved her. Really loved her. Her name was... Yes. Right. Esme. The woman they were doing this for was Esme. Esme Scott. Cheryl hadn't dressed up for him. She had no feelings for him and he had no feelings for her.

He had to remember that. Or he wouldn't survive the night.

CHAPTER EIGHTEEN

She had to survive the night. Just one night and then it would all be over. Bryant had been unusually quiet on the drive to the downtown hotel where Scott Designs was hosting a launch party for a new explorer toy. He'd been even more reserved when they entered the ballroom, bright with crystal chandeliers and accented by floor to ceiling windows, as if he were building a wall around himself. He'd said he wasn't nervous, but she didn't believe him. He probably didn't believe she could convince Esme they were a real couple.

He had a right to worry. She was worried too. Worried that she was taking this too seriously. She didn't have to pretend that he made her heart race, made her mouth run dry. She didn't have to pretend wanting to stay close to him.

If only he didn't look so good. How could a man dressed all in black make it look sexy every time? He reminded her of her black 145-piece home repair tool kit.

And she loved her tools.

A good looking black man with gray hair, a thin mustache and a face that seemed a little familiar approached them. "Bryant, I wasn't sure you'd come."

"You know I always mix business and pleasure."

"The distribution for this toy went through because of you. I hope you know how valuable you are to the company."

"It's a pleasure."

"Esme—"

"No need to worry, I don't plan on going anywhere. I keep my public and private life separate."

"She'll come to her senses."

"I'd like to introduce you to Cheryl."

The older man blinked as if she'd appeared out of nowhere. Clearly she hadn't been of any significance to him before. She tried not to hold a grudge. She was used to people like him. She'd build their houses and they'd never let her in the front door. But he graciously shook her hand. "A pleasure to meet you. What company do you work for?"

"Whelan Builders."

His eyes lit up. "Never heard of them. What's their specialty?"

"She's in construction," Bryant clarified.

She saw his interest fade. "I see."

"And she's with me."

The older man's interest returned with a different sheen. Cheryl could see the questions in his eyes when he glanced at Bryant. It then turned to disbelief before it settled into suspicion. "Esme came alone."

Bryant nodded, but didn't reply.

He looked at something behind them. "Don't let me keep you. Enjoy yourselves," he said then left.

"Who was that?" Cheryl asked.

"Marlon Scott. Esme's father."

"No wonder he looked familiar. He didn't believe us."

"Only because he doesn't want to. He really wants me to marry into the family. He thinks that's the one way to keep me."

She studied him, curious. "Are you thinking of leaving the company?"

"No, I like what I do too much and I've put too much into the company to leave it because of a misunderstanding."

"He doesn't seem sure."

"We're not here to assure him. We're here to make Esme realize what she lost."

"I haven't seen her."

"She's here," Bryant said certain. "She's keeping her distance. She does that well. She likes to slip in and out of crowds unobserved. But I always know where she is."

Cheryl looked around the room. "Do you see her now?"

"Yes." Bryant cupped her chin and gently turned her face to his, stepping closer and lowering his voice. "Look at me. You're doing great. No, don't back away from me. Stay exactly where you are."

For a moment she wanted to do the exact opposite. She didn't want to stay, she wanted to run. Run away from him; from how he made her feel. These feelings were familiar yet strange all at once and they sent her senses spinning. And her senses were being overwhelmed by the sight of his dark brows, the harsh cut of his jaw, the fullness of his lower lip; the intoxicating scent of his skin, the deep sound of his voice, the gentle touch of his fingers against her face. Then there were his eyes. Dark brown eyes that could hold her still with the tiniest of effort. They could paralyze her, excite her, seduce her.

A soft smile teased his mouth. "You're looking nervous. Relax. She's looking right at us with an expression I've never seen before." He lifted his gaze and stared past her. "This is really working."

It was working too well. This pretence felt all too real. She didn't like being this close to him. She never thought it would have bothered her before but now her body felt like it was on fire and they were barely touching and he wasn't even looking at her.

He was looking at another woman, desiring another woman and she was just a prop. She flexed her hand. It wasn't his fault. She had no right to be angry at him. That wouldn't make sense. This was why she was here. This was what they both wanted. She had to play her role. She was supposed to make Esme jealous. Not feel jealous herself.

But she was jealous. Jealous that he would have his happy ending and she never would.

By the end of the evening everything would be back to normal. She'd have him as just her tenant again and they'd barely see each other. There would be no more dinners or desserts. No more talks. No more teasing grins. No more chances to get to know him more.

That thought depressed her a little, but she pushed it aside. It was better this way. Now she wouldn't get distracted by the scent of chocolate on his clothes, the sound of his footsteps as he came into the kitchen eager for a meal or the light touch of his hand when he touched her chin as he did only a few moments ago.

She mentally shook her head. Once she knew he wouldn't leave she really needed to find at least two more tenants. It wasn't healthy for just the two of them in the large house. At least if Ginnie came out of her room more it would help, but she still stayed inside like a hermit.

Bryant took her hand and began to walk. "Come on."

"Where?"

"We're going to dance."

"Why?"

"It's what people do." He stopped and pulled her into a dancer's embrace. "And it looks better than just standing around talking."

Cheryl followed his lead, ignoring her racing pulse then she bit her lip as a sinking realization came over her. She cleared her throat then said, "You've never held a woman before."

She felt him stiffen and silently swore knowing she'd said the wrong thing.

"I've been with women," he said in a dark voice.

She tried to soften her tone. "I'm not suggesting you're a virgin."

His tone turned ironic. "Then what are you suggesting?"

"I said you've never held a woman. I didn't say you've never slept with one."

"There's a difference?"

"One's easier than the other."

"You know this from experience?"

"That came out wrong. Okay, forget the implication. Let me try again. Have you danced with a woman before?"

"If I say 'yes', you'll think I'm lying."

"If you say 'yes' I'll assume it was in the sixth grade."

"Fine." He stopped moving. "We don't need to dance then."

She didn't let him pull away. This was her chance to help him and focus on something else beside her latent lust. "No, this is a good idea. We just need to improve it a little."

He groaned and muttered, "I bet you give orders during sex."

She pretended not to hear him. "This will also help you with Esme in the future."

"I never danced with Esme."

She stared at him surprised. "Really?"

He narrowed his eyes as if ready for a challenge. "Yes."

"Then this is great. When you do dance with her on your wedding day you'll know what to do. Now listen closely. A man has three options when it comes to holding a woman. He can hold her lightly, like she's so fragile she's going to break; he can hold her too tight like she's going to run away or he can hold her like a groping octopus."

"A groping octopus?"

"Yes, like he wants to take her on the dance floor."

He nodded. "Your arithmetic is off."

"Arithmetic?"

"You just gave me three bad options. I'm assuming there's a fourth that's," he lightened his voice to mimic a little girl's, "just right," before he returned his voice to normal and said, "and if there is a fourth option you should have said a man has four options. Although I'm sure there are a fifth or sixth somewhere."

Cheryl shook her head. "Forget about the numbers. Focus on what I'm trying to say. The last—"

"Fourth. It can't be the last when there are possibly other options that—"

"Fine. The *fourth* option is a heavy, strong grip not too possessive and tight so a woman can't breathe, but sure and confident enough so the woman knows exactly where you want her to be."

He glanced past her and said in a low voice, "Right now I want her to be as far away from me as possible."

Cheryl gritted her teeth, knowing he was referring to her. Yes, this was the Bryant she had to remember. The one who'd killed her azaleas and threatened to make her pay if she didn't help him win Esme back. He wasn't the man for her at all. "Pretend she's someone else."

"I'm trying, but it's easier when she's not talking."

Cheryl stopped moving ready to give him a cutting reply, but when his gaze met hers, her mouth went dry. His eyes were bright with amusement. He'd been teasing her!

She pushed him away. "You snake."

He blinked with innocence. "What?"

"You *do* know how to dance."

He pulled her close again. "But I still need more practice."

She struggled to free herself. "Let go."

"Don't wiggle like that or you'll get me excited."

"Why do you like teasing me?"

He bit his lip. "Stop it," he said his voice urgent. "I mean it. Relax. The song will end soon."

Cheryl released an annoyed sigh and stopped trying to pull away. "Why did you hold me so close the first time?"

He lowered his gaze and when he spoke his voice was barely a whisper. "Because I briefly forgot myself."

"What does that mean?"

His eyes came up to study her face. "What do you think that means?"

Cheryl opened her mouth, but no words came out.

"You two look intense," Esme said.

CHAPTER NINETEEN

Cheryl tore her gaze away and stared at the other woman in a semi-daze, taking in Esme's black cocktail dress and gold earrings. "I'm sorry?"

"I'm not sure if you're arguing or not."

"We're not," Bryant said in a cool voice.

Esme sent him a considering look. "I'm surprised to see you here."

"You know I'd never miss this."

"I was talking to your...date."

Cheryl noticed the pause. She was ready to make sure that Esme didn't question them as a couple. "It surprised me too," Cheryl said in a bright tone. "But Bryant invited me and I couldn't say no."

"I guess your feelings about him have changed?"

"More than you know."

"Excuse me," Bryant said. "There's someone I have to talk to." He bent over and whispered in Cheryl's ear as he walked passed. "This is your chance. Talk me up."

She was glad for the reminder. The heated look he'd just given her only seconds ago had rattled her mind. It must have been her imagination or his way of teasing her. Why did he have to tease her like that! That was reason enough to hate him. The jerk. She had to focus. She had to remember why she was here. She knew what she'd come to do.

"I thought you didn't like him," Esme said, watching Bryant make his way over to an Asian woman wearing a silver dress.

"That's exactly what I wanted you to think."

Esme turned sharply to her. "What?"

"The real reason I came here was to thank you."

"Thank me?"

"For making it so easy for me to get him. I really didn't think you'd fall for my act."

Esme blinked fast. "That wasn't an act. I saw your face at the party and I listened to every word. And when I saw you again at the coffee shop you looked desperate to get me to take him back."

Cheryl nodded. "I'm glad you still think so."

"I don't think so. I *know* so. I know how to read people and there's no way you could have tricked me—"

"I didn't trick you," Cheryl interrupted with a slight shake of her head. "You had uncertain feelings about him and I just well...used that to my advantage. No hard feelings. You really are better off without him."

Esme narrowed her eyes. "I don't believe you. You didn't know who I was and Bryant is not the kind of man—"

"I don't think you even know the kind of man Bryant

is. You told me he's a hard man to read. But that's not true because I find it real easy to figure out what he's thinking and right now what's clear to me is that he's over you and he wants me."

Esme folded her arms. "Don't be fooled. You may think you're someone different now, but that will change. With him it starts off that way, as if he'll let you in and then a wall goes up."

Cheryl couldn't stop a smile. "I'm in construction, honey." She winked. "I know how to make walls come down."

CHAPTER TWENTY

*E*sme paced the hall.

She didn't like being tricked. Seeing Bryant with that woman had been a shock.

That *woman*. What was her name again? Cheryl. Cheryl something. It didn't matter. She'd been suspicious of her when she'd shown up at Bryant's office. That had never happened before. And why had he invited her to such an important event? It had been only a month. It wasn't like him to find someone else so quickly. She hadn't found anyone yet and she'd been the one to turn him down. Wasn't he supposed to be upset about their breakup?

She bit her nail.

Maybe he was. Maybe this was his revenge. He knew that showing up to the party with another woman would upset her parents. It made her look bad. Yes, he was trying to get back at her, that was all.

But Cheryl said it had been her plan all along.

Esme bit her nail harder. That woman! How could she think to try to outsmart her? She'd graduated top of her class in both high school and college. She spoke three languages, had traveled to at least thirty countries, dined with diplomats and scholars. How could she not have seen what that woman was up to? How could she be defeated by a woman who worked in construction?

Cheryl was no good. Dangerous. If she couldn't read a woman like that then Bryant was definitely in trouble. Cheryl could manipulate a man who was on the rebound.

Esme stopped pacing, coming to a decision. She may not want to marry him, but she still cared about him. He needed to be warned.

She saw him talking to Marie, making the younger woman smile, and walked over to him. "Could I borrow him for a moment," she said with a smile, taking Bryant's arm. Once they were alone she released him and said, "I was just talking to Cheryl."

"I know," he said. His voice was soft but it still gave her goose bumps and she didn't know why. He looked calm. He always looked calm when there were other people around, he was very careful to guard his features. It frustrated her because she'd moved them far enough away from anyone else so that no one could overhear them. He was safe to let his mask drop.

But it remained in place and she couldn't read what he was thinking. That had always bothered her the most. She couldn't tell if he was happy to talk to her or annoyed. Was he hurt? Angry? Resentful? He stared at her as if he'd filed their relationship away in a folder called "the past" and treated her as he would any other colleague. On the one hand she was grateful (she didn't want any drama), but on another it bothered her that he was so devoid of extreme emotion.

But she knew he was a decent guy and didn't want to see him get used. "I'm telling you this because I still care about you, but you'd better be careful."

"Of what?"

"Cheryl."

His expression didn't change, but he sounded interested. "Why?"

"She's not what she seems. She lies."

"She hasn't lied to me."

"Just be careful. Rebound relationships can be—"

The corner of his mouth kicked up in a grin. "I know how to look after myself."

"I wouldn't have thought she was your type."

"You don't know much about me then." He stepped closer and lowered his voice, his eyes piercing hers. "But let me tell you a few things you may have missed. I don't hold a grudge and I'm open to taking chances."

Esme stared at him speechless. He looked like a new man. A dangerously sexy man. She'd never seen this Bryant before. A Bryant wound up with pent up heat searching for release. Even when they'd been together he'd never looked at her that way.

"Chances?" she said, her voice coming out in a squeak. She felt heat creeping up her neck. "Like second chances?"

Bryant let his gaze rove slowly over her body then met her eyes. "Are you offering?"

She steadied her voice. "No."

He nodded. "Good, because I've moved on. I suggest you do the same. But thanks for worrying about me." He offered a soft, indulgent smile. "That's sweet." He turned and walked away.

Esme watched him leave and leaned against the wall to keep herself from collapsing. He'd made her knees feel like jelly. Who was that man? Bryant had never looked or spoken to her like that before. Cheryl was right, Bryant did have sexy hidden depths, she hadn't seen them. Why not? Was Cheryl the reason for this change in him?

Sweet? He'd called her sweet?

Nobody called her sweet. She was gorgeous. Brilliant. Amazing.

She pounded the wall with her fist. She didn't like to be upstaged by anyone. She wasn't sure she wanted him back, but he had been in love with her. Shouldn't he show that? He couldn't have gotten over her that quickly.

How could he have asked her to marry him only a month ago and then date another woman? His landlady no less. It was embarrassing. Her mother would never let her live this down. It would be different if he'd chosen someone else. Someone more suitable. Someone more worthy of envy. Not some stocky woman who wanted to brag that she'd stolen Esme's man away.

She didn't like to be embarrassed and she wouldn't be. She'd find someone else for Bryant. She may not want him, but she wouldn't let Cheryl have him either. She would out maneuver her.

Esme tapped her chin as another thought came to her. Or she could ask Bryant to give her a second chance. That would please her mother, relieve her father and set things right.

Esme left the party with that strategy in mind. How would Cheryl feel if she really had competition? Bryant may have had his pride hurt, but they had history and history counted for something. They made a great team, they could make a marriage work and she could grow to love him.

Esme returned home, took a long hot shower then wrapped a towel around herself and opened the closet.

She screamed.

A large, bearded black man stared at her.

He held up his hands. "Sorry, I was told nobody would be here for another couple hours."

Once she composed herself she recognized who he was. The man her mother had hired to redesign her closet. She'd seen him in passing but had never paid close attention. She did now and liked what she saw. He was big and beautifully built.

"The rest of the team has gone home and I just wanted to look over a few things. I have written permission—"

"It's okay. I was shocked. I thought I was alone."

"You didn't see my truck outside?"

Clearly she wasn't herself. "No."

"Oh," he said, keeping his gaze on her face and she knew the reason why. She was only wrapped in a towel. He was interested but trying to be a gentleman. An attractive man admiring her attributes always made her feel better.

He cleared his throat. "I'm almost done."

She even liked his voice. It was big and broad like him. She walked over to him. "No, rush." She took her satin robe from off a hook and put it on. "Take your time." She looked at a new shelf he'd been measuring. She let her finger trail the length of it.

"Thanks," he said. "But I—"

"It's late. Your wife must be anxious to know where you are."

"I don't have a wife."

"Girlfriend/Boyfriend?"

He shook his head, his eyes amused. "No."

Esme began to grin. "What's your name?"

"Shawn. Shawn Whelan."

She held out her hand. "I'm sorry I haven't had a chance to introduce myself before. I'm Esme Scott."

"Nice to meet you." He shook her hand. His hand was rough, but that only thrilled her more. He wasn't her type at all, but two could play at this game. If Bryant wanted a construction worker, she'd have a contractor.

"Would you like something to drink?" she asked him.

"Um..."

"It's okay. I just want the company. I don't want to be alone tonight and I'll make it worth your time. I have a lot of friends and I'd be happy to recommend you."

She adjusted her robe and saw his eyes heat up. It cheered her. She still had the touch. That was important. To think that she'd been tossed aside for someone like Cheryl had bruised her pride.

After two drinks she'd gotten a French kiss and after three she was over her humiliation completely. She threw away any thought of reuniting with Bryant. She was going to have a little fun of her own.

CHAPTER TWENTY-ONE

"Have you seen Esme?" Mrs. Scott asked Bryant, stopping him on his way to rejoin Cheryl.

"No, but I spoke to her a couple of minutes ago."

"I see."

He nodded then began to move past her. Mrs. Scott made him uneasy. She reminded him of a water gun. The ones that looked too real. They were innately a harmless fun toy, but could still get you killed if seen in the wrong light. He liked to keep his distance. But she hindered his escape by resting a light hand on his arm. "I hope you don't think that it's over."

"Over?"

"You know that Esme can get into certain...moods. This is merely one of them. I'm afraid this is probably my fault. I was a little overeager for this engagement to happen. I wouldn't be surprised if she turned you down to get back at me."

Bryant sniffed. "I don't think Esme is spiteful."

"She has her moments. I just wanted you to know that."

"I've moved on."

"It would be best if you were a little," she paused, "more patient. It doesn't do our company image much good to see you so quickly moving on to someone else. Especially someone out of nowhere."

"I don't believe my personal life has anything to do with the company image."

She flashed a tight smile. "That's where you are wrong. My husband wants to keep this business within the family. We want someone we can trust. Although you are very important to us, you might find it hard to rise to a certain," she paused again, "position that we are saving for someone willing to join our ranks. Am I making myself clear?"

"Too clear," he said in a grim tone.

"You and Esme are a perfect pair. I hope you don't let her little rebellion get in the way of your ambition. You can go very far with the right connections."

He nodded.

She nodded too and smiled like a plastic doll. "So glad we had this little chat."

Cheryl was sipping a sparkling drink and laughing with a man who was telling her the history of GI Joe when Byrant approached her. He looked like thunder. The other man saw his face and quickly faded away.

Cheryl set her glass down afraid she would drop it. "What did I do wrong?"

He blinked. "What?"

"You had that same expression on your face when you accused me of ruining your life. You talked about strangling me."

He sighed and rubbed his forehead. "I'm not angry at you. At least not right now."

That was a relief. "I saw you talking to Esme before." She search the crowd to find her. "Didn't it go well?"

"It went very well."

She turned to him confused. "You don't sound happy about that."

"I'm happy."

"You don't look like it."

He clenched his jaw. "I am. I am very happy."

"Are you ready to leave?"

He nodded.

She wrapped her arm around his. It felt as tight as a coiled snake. "Can I ask what happened to make you so...um...happy?"

He kept walking.

Once they were outside in the hall, she spun around, shoved him against the wall and kissed him. She drew away and met his startled gaze. "Now you can be angry at me. Or at least tell me what's wrong with you."

"You think kissing me will make me angry?" he said in a flat tone.

"You don't like me touching you."

"Yes, that's right," he said in a low growl before he

pushed himself from the wall and covered her mouth with his.

She shoved him back, breathless, her heart pounding. His kiss had been wild and intoxicating. "What are you doing?"

"Being angry with you." He trailed a series of warm kisses down her neck. "Very. Very angry."

"I was trying to distract you," she said, feeling slightly dizzy when she felt the tip of his wet tongue touch her skin.

"It's working," he said in a deep tone before he captured her mouth again.

Cheryl's mind told her to pull away, that she didn't want to be the object of his anger. But his kiss felt anything but angry, it felt insistent, hungry and searching. It felt delicious and called to something deep within her. His hands slipped up her arms, bringing her closer. Her shawl fell to the ground and she felt his hard body against hers. And he was hard everywhere. She ached to be closer, to wrap her legs around him and feel him inside her.

"No," she cried, turning her face away. "We can't do this here."

"Why not? No one's looking."

Cheryl pulled away from him and held her hand up. She had to be the sensible one even though her mind was spinning. "Tell me what happened. Did Esme turn you down?"

Bryant stared at her mouth and licked his lip as if he'd finished a fine meal and wanted more. He nodded.

His heated gaze made her skin tingle, she fought to stay on topic. "And you're upset about that?"

He nodded again.

Cheryl bent down and picked up her shawl with trembling fingers. "We'll come up with another plan. But it can't be this."

"Why not?" He rested his hands on her waist, his gaze bright with fire. "I like being angry with you."

He didn't look angry. He looked...like a man gazing at an object of desire. But that couldn't be right. He'd been with Esme only a few minutes ago. He was angry, she had to remember that. He was using her as a substitute for what he really wanted. She held him back. "I know you're upset with Esme and I'm supposed to help you, but I won't let you take it out on me."

"You kissed me first." Bryant took her shawl from her hand and slowly draped it around her shoulders. "And I warned you about touching me."

He was right, she'd gotten a response she hadn't been prepared for. She was still shaken. "I'm sorry. I was wrong."

Bryant released a long sigh, his dark gaze never leaving her face.

Cheryl lowered her gaze no longer able to meet his. "We should go."

He drew her close and embraced her. "This isn't your fault."

Cheryl blinked too stunned to move, fighting not to sink into his arms. "What are you doing?"

He sighed again. "I'm not angry at you or Esme."

"Then what's wrong?"

"I don't like being told what to do."

"But I didn't—"

"I know." He released her and said in a quiet voice, "But someone else is trying to." He tapped his chest, his tone turned hard. "I went out with Esme because I liked her. I wasn't thinking about my job."

Cheryl nodded not understanding the reason for his renewed anger. "I know that."

"I'm not the kind of man who picks a woman in order to help his career. I don't need anyone's help."

Cheryl nodded again not knowing what else to say.

"So why do they think that I asked her to marry me because..." He looked away in frustration. "I loved...love her. That's why I wanted...want to marry her." He returned his gaze to hers, his eyes searching for understanding. "There's no other reason."

"I know," Cheryl said softly. "I believe you."

"Then why don't they?"

"Who?"

Bryant shook his head. "Never mind. You can relax." He shoved his hands into his pockets and marched towards the exit. "Everything worked tonight. She tried to warn me off you."

Cheryl hurried to keep up with him. "Okay," Cheryl said, surprised he didn't make it sound like good news. "That means you should hear from her soon."

He nodded looking grim. "Right. She'll want a second chance."

Bryant held the door open for her and as she walked

through it the spring breeze brushed her skin, but did little to cool it. She still felt too warm. "And that's good," she said no longer certain.

"Right." He sent her a hooded gaze. "You don't have to worry about losing a tenant."

CHAPTER TWENTY-TWO

She should be able to sleep.

She shouldn't be sitting in her kitchen wondering why she felt miserable. She'd succeeded. She should feel triumphant. Cheryl sat at her kitchen table and looked around the empty room. Memories of Martin mingled beside memories of Bryant. Bryant by the sink, Bryant setting the table, Bryant taking a taste of her soup. He wouldn't make any more requests. He didn't need to. He was getting his darling Esme back.

She couldn't believe he'd be in love with such a fickle woman. If he'd been hers no one would have been able to change her mind about him. But he wasn't hers and she didn't need him to be. One love was enough. One love that nearly destroyed her. She was finally feeling human again; she couldn't do anything to threaten that.

"You couldn't sleep either?"

She spun around and saw Bryant in the doorway. She tampered down her joy. "You owe me an apology."

He sat in front of her. "Is that what's keeping you up?"

"Yes," she lied.

He sighed. "Why?"

"What do you mean 'Why?' Do you think I enjoyed you taking out your frustration on me?"

"Yes. Very much."

She surged to her feet, outraged. "What?"

He gestured to her chair. "Shh. You'll wake up the house."

"Ginnie won't come down. What do you mean—?"

He shook his head, suddenly looking tired. "Forget it. Sit down. I'm sorry."

She slowly sat down, not taking her eyes off him as if he were a sleeping lion. "You're in a really strange mood. Are you usually like this after a party? If so no wonder—" She stopped.

His gaze sharpened. "No wonder what?"

"Never mind."

"No wonder Esme dumped me?"

"No, I wasn't going to say that."

"What were you going to say?"

She bit her lip. "One time I saw you in the main room watching the live action Transformers movie. You were dressed the way you are now and I thought it strange that you hadn't changed. You stared at the screen but you didn't look like you were enjoying it."

"I see."

"What is it about these parties that you hate?"

"It's not the parties it's..." He sat back. "People think I'm ambitious."

"Aren't you?"

"Not the way they think. I work hard. I play hard. I like to win, but I don't use other people to get an advantage. That's not who I am. Even though that's what some people think."

"Transformers...more than meets the eye," she said remembering their tag line.

Bryant couldn't stop a smile. "I know there's a psychological connection there, but I'm not in the mood."

"If it makes you feel good."

"I didn't think the movie would wake you."

"It didn't. It was on mute."

He shrugged. "I already knew the story."

"We designed the house to absorb noise so you couldn't have woken me anyway. I was already up at that time."

"You could have joined me."

"You looked like you wanted to be alone."

He nodded resigned. "People tend to think that too."

Cheryl paused. "But you don't want to be alone?"

"No. I don't."

"Does Esme know that?"

He hesitated. "I thought she did."

"You have to tell her how you feel. She doesn't always feel certain."

He pulled on his ear. "I still don't understand that. You know how I feel, right?"

More than you know. "Yes, but you're different with me."

"How?"

"I don't know. But the man Esme describes and the man you are seem to be two different people."

"What did she say about me?"

"That you have a wall. That you're easygoing at first and then you're hard to get to know."

Bryant rested his chin in his hand, pensive. "She's right. I'm careful with her."

"Why?"

"Because she needs me to be. She's been raised by two critical parents, her mother more than her father. I know that I can outshine her at work and she's used to being the best. She had a blow to her confidence a couple years back because of a poor business decision, but I've been helping her get over it. I don't want to intimidate her. And I don't want her to think that I'm after anything but her. She's been burned by other guys in the past."

"But after two years you should be able to be yourself."

He sat up. "I am myself. I like being with her."

She kicked him under the table.

He winced and glared at her. She grinned and pointed at his face. "Has Esme ever seen that expression?"

"No," Bryant said through clenched teeth. He rubbed his shin. "I told you. I *like* being with her." He narrowed his gaze and kicked her chair with enough force it titled backwards.

Cheryl grabbed the table to keep from toppling over then laughed. "Lucky her. Does she know you watch action movies like the Transformers without the sound when you're mad?"

He looked away.

"Or the real reason why you like to design toys?"

He looked at her. "I haven't even told you that."

"I know and the fact that you haven't told her says a lot." She fluttered her lashes. "Since you *like* being with her."

"It says that I'm smart."

"What's smart about that?"

"I don't want to bore her. I like to design toys because I like to play with toys. It's as simple as that."

"Okay."

"I didn't have a tragic childhood if that's what you're thinking. I wasn't raised by cruel parents who kept me in a black room with no toys so that I decided I'd make them as an adult."

"I said okay. I don't want to know."

"I don't believe you." Bryant rested his chin in his hand and studied her. "I have a request."

"You can think about food right now?"

He nodded. "Cookies."

She glanced at the clock. It was nearly twelve. "This late?"

"You have something better to do?"

"It's late."

"You've already said that. Come on. It will be the last time."

"Esme will make the next round?"

Bryant leaned back and shook his head. "I told you she doesn't bake."

"I'm sure she will if you ask her. Does she know about your sweet tooth?"

He walked over to a cupboard and opened it.

Cheryl frowned as he pulled out a large mixing bowl. "What are you doing?"

"Getting the things you need to bake the cookies."

"You're really bent on them, aren't you?"

He glanced over his shoulder with an impish grin. "Aren't you?"

Cheryl pushed her chair back and stood. "I shouldn't since you kicked my chair."

"You kicked me first."

He was right. Plus it would be a nice distraction. And it would be the last time. She didn't want to waste it.

Nearly an hour later the scent of sugar, flour and chocolate chips filled the warm kitchen. "This is nice," Bryant said, sitting at the table, biting into one of the cookies.

"Hmm."

"Once a month. We should do this."

"Like a tradition."

"Something like that."

"You might be too busy," Cheryl said.

"I doubt it. That's the one thing with Esme, she fits into my life perfectly."

"That's not easy to find." She knew how hard it could be. There had never been anything perfect about her life or schedule with Martin. When she was with her previous employer she remembered early mornings and long days. When she started the business with Martin, the days had been even longer and at times stressful even when things were going well. They'd learned to prioritize time together and that hadn't always been easy. But it had been fun and worth it. It made the time they were together extra special because it took effort.

Her life with Bryant wouldn't fit perfectly. When she was in the middle of a new project, she would be exhausted. There wouldn't be meals like this. She wouldn't be able to always make it to fancy parties if she'd spent the previous day on a major project. And most of the people at the parties spoke a different language about an industry she knew nothing about. She didn't belong there.

Esme wouldn't have to make many changes for Bryant. They did fit well together.

"What will you do once my year lease is up?" Bryant asked her.

She didn't want to think about him leaving, even though she knew it was inevitable. "I'll get other renters. I've just been busy, but I know this place will suit a lot of people."

He fell silent a moment then said, "When you're ready for more roommates let me know. I can make a few calls."

Cheryl didn't know what to say. She knew he was right. He knew she wasn't ready yet, but wasn't ready to admit it either. "Thanks. Finding the right tenants isn't exactly easy."

"Hmm," he said and she was glad he didn't say anything else. Allowing her to pretend that he'd swallowed her lie. He pushed the plate of cookies away and sat back. "That was delicious."

"You're not going to eat the entire batch?"

He feigned a look of hurt. "I'm saving some for Hannah."

"Good. It'll be my last batch for a while. I'll be busy. We're starting a new building project. The Kent's dream house. Breaking ground always take up a lot of work and —" She stopped because she knew she was talking too much. She stood. "We should go to bed." She paused when she realized what she'd just said. "I mean together." She shook her head, her face burning. "Separately. We should go to bed separately. To sleep."

A flash of humor crossed his face. "I know."

"Goodnight," she said then raced out of the kitchen glad that he was now Esme's problem.

She soon discovered she was wrong.

CHAPTER TWENTY-THREE

Cheryl walked into her office and stopped when she saw a couple kissing in front of Shawn's desk. She backed up shocked. Shawn had his ladies but he rarely had them over in the office. "Oh, excuse me," she said then hurried out. She would scold him later, but right now she didn't want to embarrass his companion. She glanced out the window and saw a silver car. A silver car with a license plate that caught her eye. TY DSGNR. Toy Designer? Ohno!

Cheryl swung the door open and stared, hoping she would be proven wrong.

"I'll get going," Esme said, giving Shawn one lingering kiss before she walked past Cheryl. "Bye."

Cheryl closed the door behind her. She struggled to keep her voice calm when she spoke. "What are you doing?"

"I left my watch at her place the other night and she stopped by to return it."

She folded her arms and tapped her foot. "And you were just thanking her?"

"That night was…It just happened."

Cheryl pointed to the door where Esme had exited. "With her! Of all the people it had to be with her!"

"In my defense, if you'd seen her in that towel—"

"I don't care if she were completely naked and she was covered in honey. She's Bryant's fiancée."

"Ex-fiancée." Shawn held his hands up in surrender. "I'm sorry but she came on to me." He stroked his beard with a wistful grin. "And now you've got that honey image stuck in my mind."

"So she came on to you. You could have said no."

"No, I couldn't. Have you seen her?" He rested a hand on his chest. "If you were in my shoes would you really turn her down?"

Cheryl gritted her teeth. "Yes, because she belongs to someone else."

Shawn shook his head in regret. "Not anymore."

"You have to break it off."

"I don't want to."

She raised her fist and shook it, her voice a warning. "If you want to live another day you will."

"I'll die a happy man. You don't understand. A guy like me doesn't get a chance like this. When I've done some jobs I've had ladies flash their tits and suntan in the nude, but when Esme sent me all the signals that she wanted company for the night, I couldn't let that chance pass."

"She's using you. Can't you see that?"

Shawn feigned a look of hurt. "You mean she just wants me for my body and not my mind?"

"This is serious."

"Not really, BB Cream. And who are you to talk? Isn't Bryant using you?"

She looked away. "It's different."

"How? Isn't he getting a little more than a fake girl-friend? How many dinners and desserts have you made? And it is really 'dessert', right?"

She shot him an ugly look even though her neck burned with the memory of the kiss they'd shared. "You are disgusting."

"I'm being honest."

"I like to cook, he likes to eat. That's all and he's not using me. It's part of a plan because I messed things up in the first place. You cannot ruin this for me. I've come too close to winning. She was jealous the other night. He can win her back. Break it off with her."

Shawn leaned against his desk and folded his arms. "She'll only find someone else."

"No, she won't because Bryant will quickly take her back and things will return to normal."

"No, they won't," he said in a quiet voice. "That's the trouble. Even if you got Bryant to stay that won't make things normal again."

"Shawn—"

"Just sell the house."

Her lips thinned. "No."

"I don't think—"

She grabbed his collar, she knew it was a useless

gesture since he was much bigger than her but she didn't care.

"I will never forgive you for this." She released him. "I hate you with the venom of a thousand snakes. Now get out of my sight."

~

Take that Cheryl!

Esme walked into the entrance of Scott Designs with a sassy stride, feeling triumphant. She'd gotten caught just as she'd hoped and the shock on Cheryl's face had been priceless. She didn't just look shocked, she looked angry. And just what would make her angry? Didn't she have a man of her own? Or was that really just an act?

She pushed the elevator button with a smile.

"What's put you in a good mood?" a familiar voice said.

She looked at Bryant who was stepping out of the down elevator. "I got some good news." She noticed his jacket and attaché case. "Is there a meeting I forgot about?"

"Nope, I'm leaving for the day."

The elevator door opened but she didn't step inside. "Are you sick?"

"No." He held the door open before it closed again. "You'd better get inside."

She stared at him confused. "Where are you going?"

He let the elevator door close. "It's personal."

"But you never leave before me. You're always the last one here."

"I'm not ignoring my duties if that's what you're worried about."

"Is it because of her? What's gotten into you? You can't wait to get home to her brownies?" She remembered the day he'd shared them with the office staff and everyone had raved about them. "I guess if I cooked for you I would have seen this side of you?"

"I've got to go." He lowered his voice. "We can talk about this later."

"Fine," she called after him as he walked away. "But I should warn you."

He turned to her. "About what?"

"She's not happy."

"Why?"

Esme hid a grin glad she'd finally gotten his full attention. "I'm seeing her contractor."

"Why would she be unhappy about that?"

"I don't know. She wasn't happy when she saw us together. She looked...jealous."

Esme waited and watched to see Bryant's face change, but he looked calm as usual. She wanted to shake him. "Doesn't that bother you?"

"That you've moved on?"

Was he really this dense? "No, that your girlfriend is jealous of me."

A knowing smile spread across his lips. "I don't think she's the one who's jealous."

Esme took a step back as if he suddenly smelled. She made a face. "Why would I be jealous of *her*?"

Bryant studied her thoughtfully for a moment. "Exactly," he said. He turned. "I'll see you later."

*E*sme was rattled.

That was good.

He should be ecstatic.

But he was worried.

Bryant rested his head on his steering wheel and groaned.

What's gotten into you? It was a good question. Esme was right. He was always last leaving work. Work had filled his life, his mind. He never had a reason to leave early. He scheduled his dates with Esme on the weekends, his weeks were always well compartmentalized. Then why was he rushing home?

Because he wanted to celebrate with her. He'd secured another distributor for one of their older products and it had been a hard won victory. He wanted to order takeaway and tell Cheryl all about it.

He'd never been so eager to go home in his life. He could have sent a text or called her on the phone. He didn't need to tell her at all. But somehow it felt right. Being with Cheryl felt right, even when she annoyed him. Or shocked him. Or teased him. She could be unpredictable and he liked that.

Maybe that's why Esme had turned him down. He'd been too predictable. She didn't like to cook, but maybe he should have surprised her on a weeknight with a dinner date. Or done something out of the ordinary. With Cheryl he saw all the ways he'd let his relationship with Esme slip through his fingers. Had he really been such a bad boyfriend? Hadn't he stood up for her at the office and made sure she was given certain projects her father meant to delegate to others?

And why was he talking about their relationship in the past tense? He could win her back. That was the whole point and she was rattled. That was good. He knew her interest in another man was just a fling. Her standards went beyond a contractor. He felt a little sorry for the guy.

Bryant straightened and started the ignition. He had to tell Cheryl what was going on.

He was going to be furious.

Cheryl checked the roasted potatoes, then stirred her sautéed red and green bell peppers, snow peas and carrots. She'd made a special meal to make the bad news seem less awful.

Bryant came into the kitchen. "What's all this?"

"Just sit down."

He held up a bag with an Italian logo. "I brought takeaway."

"Oh."

"But we'll save it for later. What's up?"

"Why should anything be up?"

He opened the fridge and placed the bag inside. "You look terrified."

She was. She set the food on the table. "I've got bad news. It's about Esme. She's—"

He washed his hands then filled up his plate. "She's seeing someone else."

She stared at him. "You knew?"

"I just found out today."

She slowly sank into her seat. "I'm so sorry."

"Why? It's not your fault."

She bit her lip. "It sort of is."

"How?"

"She's seeing Shawn."

He frowned. "Shawn?"

"My brother-in-law."

"Oh...*that* contractor," Bryant said with a laugh.

Cheryl blinked. Did he find this funny? Maybe he was so shocked he was trying to pretend it didn't hurt. "I'm sure she's confused. I bet she wants you to be jealous of her."

"Hmm." He took a bite of a sliced bell pepper and closed his eyes. "You're spoiling me."

Cheryl watched him uncertain of his mood. "You don't have to pretend you're not upset."

"I'm not upset."

She paused. He didn't sound upset, he looked...

relieved. But perhaps he was so hungry he wasn't really listening to her. "I have a new plan. I think if you go after her then—"

"I don't want to."

"What?"

"I don't want to do this anymore."

Cheryl jumped to her feet. She knew he had been taking it too well. Fortunately, she had another plan. "You don't mean that." She opened the fridge and pulled out a pie. "I knew you'd be disappointed so I baked you this. Let me warm it up."

"It looks delicious. Put it away. I'll get to it later."

"But I—"

"Sit down."

She put the pie away, sat down and rubbed her hands on her jeans. "If you give me a little more time. I know the three months aren't over yet, but this complicates things and—"

He shook his head, sounding tired. "Stop it, Cheryl."

"Bryant, please—"

He sighed. "I can't give you more time."

"Why not?"

"Because I don't want to."

Pain shot through her heart. He was going to leave her. And for the first time she didn't think about the extra income she'd lose. She'd lose a friend too. She'd failed him. "Please don't say that."

He set his fork down and stood. "Why not? It's the truth. I don't want her anymore."

Cheryl felt her mouth go dry, her throat tightened with fear and loss. Was he going to pack up his bags and leave tonight? This moment? She jumped to her feet and pressed her hands together in a plea. "Bryant—"

"It's no use." He walked around the table and stood in front of her. "I want someone else."

She stared at him stunned. "You want me to help you get someone else?"

He nodded.

"Who?"

"The woman I'm looking at right now," he said before he gathered her into his arms and kissed her.

CHAPTER TWENTY-FIVE

She needed that kiss. A kiss that told her he wasn't going to leave. That he wanted to stay with her. A kiss that gave her the courage to breathe again to feel desire fully again. And it also filled her with pain and longing. She hadn't felt an aching desire like this in so long. She hadn't felt anything and the power of her feelings—relief, joy, arousal—threatened to overwhelm her. Tears touched her eyes.

"Shh," Bryant said gently, pulling back. "It's okay." He took a deep, steadying breath. "This isn't what I expected either." He turned away, to her relief. She didn't want him to see the tears gathering in her eyes. She quickly blinked them away. This wasn't supposed to happen. How had he managed to find the key to her heart?

She started to shake and couldn't stop.

"Shh," he said again, his voice even more tender than before. "It's okay."

She bit her lip. It didn't feel okay. He wasn't looking at her. Why wasn't he looking at her? Was he avoiding her gaze? Did he want to pretend that it hadn't happened? Maybe he'd tell her that it was on impulse, that he was frustrated, that he'd wished she was Esme instead and...

His gaze met hers, a lethal calmness in his eyes and voice. "I don't want to hurt you."

But he would. He was using her again, just as he had the night of the party. Get a hold of yourself Cheryl. It was nothing. Only a kiss. He didn't mean it when he said he wanted her. She steeled herself ready for his words.

"But I really want to kiss you again."

She blinked and before she could reply he did. And the kiss was even better than before. No, no, this was wrong. How could he? How could she? They were supposed to have a plan. She was only supposed to want him as a tenant. Not as a man. She didn't need a man. Her life was fine as it was.

But her body told her that she wanted more. Much more. This time she pulled away, her hands pressed against his chest. That's enough, she wanted to tell him, but her mouth wouldn't move and she could feel his heart pounding. Pounding as much as hers. And it felt good.

She swallowed and stared at the ground. Tomorrow this would be a memory. She needed to step back and...

Bryant drew her into his arms and held her tight. "Don't be frightened," he whispered, his breath warm against her ear. "I told you I don't want to hurt you."

"I know."

"You're still shaking."

She took a deep breath. "I'll stop in a minute."

"And I don't want you to stare at me like that."

"Like what?"

He drew back and met her eyes. "Like I'll break your heart."

A sob caught in her throat and tears filled her eyes. He knew too much. It would hurt to care for someone again. He wouldn't mean to, but he could hurt her and she didn't want to hurt again.

He smoothed her hair then caressed her cheek. "I want to be with you. Give me a chance."

"I don't know." She shook her head as tears streamed down her face. Her heart screaming *Yes, yes, I want to be with you too.* But her mind reminding her of the pain of loss.

"We'll go slowly."

She sniffed and wiped the tears away. "You love Esme."

"And you love Martin." He hesitated. "I think together we can learn to love someone else. I'm willing to try if you are."

She swallowed, wanting to hold onto him and push him away at the same time. "I'm not sure."

Bryant nodded and drew away. "When you're ready, I'll be waiting."

He'd only meant to tell her his good news, not express how he really felt about her.

Bryant lay on his bed and stared up at the ceiling.

He didn't know what he was doing. No, that was wrong. He knew *exactly* what he was doing, he just wasn't sure if it was the right thing to do. The timing was all wrong. He'd used a widowed woman to get his ex back and had ended up falling for her? How did that make him look?

Like a pathetic loser.

He sat up and swore. He didn't care how it looked, he wasn't going back. This felt right. When he learned Esme was with someone else he'd felt relieved. He didn't want to think about her anymore. He wanted to move on with someone else and that person was Cheryl.

He had to give her some time to get used to the idea.

She still loves her husband, you don't have a prayer.

Bryant walked over to his window and stared down at the driveway that had once been bracketed by azaleas. But although the azaleas were gone the memory of them still lingered since nothing had been put in their place.

He knew the feelings she had for her husband were still strong. It was one of the reasons he'd decided to rent the room from her in the first place, he felt sorry for her and she looked like she needed the help. Not that she'd ever admit it.

And would she admit that she wanted him? The way her body responded to him, told him yes, but he wasn't sure she'd ever have the courage to say the words.

Martin built buildings, you build toys.

Bryant swore. He didn't like the odds. They didn't lean in his favor. He knew he had to be patient, but he didn't want to be. He wanted to be with her now. He wanted to start building a new future.

She appreciated what he was doing. Bryant was allowing her to set the pace. He wasn't coming on too strong, he was being considerate.

She hated that.

Cheryl finished cleaning up the dinner dishes and headed up stairs. She didn't want him to be so controlled. She wanted him to take the lead, so that she wouldn't have to think, couldn't think, then she could place all the responsibility on him.

She wanted to be overwhelmed with emotions so that her rational mind couldn't protest. She wanted slow, hot kisses, his hands around her, his body against hers. She didn't want to think about Esme or Martin or anything.

Cheryl stood in front of his door. She wanted it all and more.

She lifted her hand to knock then stopped.

He was also giving her a chance to turn back. To change her mind. Would he let her do that? What would he say if she said it had all been a mistake? Should she say that? Stop it now before she slipped in deeper? Did she really want a new relationship that would risk her heart again?

She closed her eyes and groaned. Yes. She wanted it too much.

She opened her eyes and looked at the ceiling. What if she waited too long and he changed his mind? What if he realized that he really was on the rebound and wanted Esme back again? How could she stand pretending her feelings for him hadn't changed?

Cheryl took a deep breath, stared at the door again and raised her hand to knock. She never thought she'd be knocking on this door. Not just because it was Bryant's, but because it had once been theirs—hers and Martin's. She feared the memories she would face inside.

The door swung open. She gasped, startled. Bryant pulled her inside and closed the door.

"I'm patient, but I'm not that patient."

"What?"

"You've been standing there for ten minutes."

"No I haven't."

He folded his arms. "It felt like an hour." He nodded to the bed.

She widened her eyes at his boldness. He shook his head. "I'll telling you to take a seat."

"Oh."

"What do you have to say?"

"You look angry."

He pulled on his ear. "This is me being nice."

"Nice?"

He nodded. "Right now I'm resisting the urged to grab and kiss you again." His hands fell to his hips. "Talk fast because my resolve is fading."

She turned and opened the door. "I should go."

"Okay."

She didn't move.

He sighed. "If you don't want this. You'd better leave now."

She slowly turned to him.

He narrowed his eyes. "I mean it."

"I know." She swallowed and closed the door behind

her. She let her gaze survey the room and all her fears vanished. The room was completely different. Bryant had made it his own. The bed was something Martin never would have chosen; he liked wood accents not black. Her gaze fell to the wood art figurine on the windowsill, the abstract painting on the wall. It freed her; there were no memories to fight only new ones to make.

His voice deepened with feeling. "You know how I feel. But if it's too soon..."

She took a step towards him.

He covered the rest, closing the distance between them. His lips brushed hers as he spoke. "Please don't regret this."

"I won't." She unbuttoned his shirt. "Promise you won't either."

"Never," he whispered. His words almost a vow. He tore off his shirt and unzipped his trousers and pulled them off.

Cheryl stared then started to laugh.

He frowned. "What?"

She covered her mouth and pointed.

"You've never seen an erection before?"

She shook her head and laughed. "It's not that. It's red. I never imagined you wearing red boxers. I thought they'd be black."

He narrowed his eyes. "Glad you find it so amusing."

She slipped out of her blouse. "Do you want to be angry with me again?" She tossed her blouse on the ground then unlatched her bra. "Very, very angry?"

His gaze heated. "You're going to drive me crazy."

She got under the covers then dropped the bra on the ground.

Bryant stared at her. "That's it? That's all I get to see?"

She wiggled out of her jeans. "Join me and you'll see more."

He lifted up the sheet. "Just let me—"

She snatched the sheet from him. "Get in bed."

"I didn't expect you to be shy."

She kicked her jeans onto the ground. "I'm not shy."

He reached for the sheets again. "Then let me see—"

She slapped his hand away. "Get in."

He folded his arms. "How can I get in when you won't even let me touch the covers?"

"Get in without looking."

He removed his boxers. "You can look at me."

"I don't care, it's not the same."

"Fine, I understand," he said resigned. He opened a drawer and slid on a condom. "You've never been with a man before."

She shot him a look.

He eased down beside her with a naughty grin. "Now there are three ways to be with a man." He reached for the sheets then pulled them back, uncovering her.

"What are you doing!" she screamed, covering her chest with her arms.

"First you can be scared of him and be as stiff as plastic."

"Plastic can melt."

He placed a finger over her lips. "Quiet, I'm giving the lesson this time."

"What else then?" She scrambled for the sheets but his body covered hers before she could. "You can become as limp as a wet piece of string. Or," he buried his face in her neck, "you can trust him."

She wanted to trust him. She glanced at the blanket then looked away, Bryant was a better option.

He was certainly a lot warmer. He smelled better too and she felt his arousal pressed against her thigh. No bed sheet had ever felt like that before.

He wrapped his arms around her and rolled on his back, reversing their positions. "Come on," he urged her. "Play with me."

It was the word "play" that unlocked her reluctance. She'd been taking it too seriously, worried about how long it had been, what he would think of her body. But play meant fun, fun meant freedom.

And like he had changed the room, something inside her changed too. He'd brought fun back into her life. The fun of cooking, the fun of dressing up, the fun of being with a man. A man who wanted her as much as she wanted him.

She looked at his lean, hard body and allowed herself to be a child again playing with her trucks in the dirt. Sliding her hands under the warm earth, letting the feel of the soil slip through her fingers. There was the same anticipation as she looked over him, touched him, explored the landscape of his form. It still amazed her how alive he made her feel.

But it scared her a little. Who was she without her

grief? Who was she without bitterness? Happiness felt strange, foreign yet familiar and it frightened her. How was it that her heart could beat for someone else, that her body could crave another man's touch?

It's okay, a voice whispered. Martin's voice. And it made her throat tighten. She knew he would want her to be happy, she knew he wouldn't want this house to be a memory of her sadness.

She didn't have to be sad anymore. She didn't have to be angry anymore. She didn't have to be alone. She hungrily took Bryant's mouth unafraid that her passion would scare him off. She did trust him. She trusted that his feelings were as real and as conflicted as hers. That they didn't need to be perfect together, they just needed to be honest. She welcomed him inside her, spreading her legs wide, inviting him in deep.

And he went deeper than her body was prepared for.

She squeezed her eyes shut against the swirling emotions. Guilt (it felt so good, so right), ecstasy (how could being alive feel so sweet and wild?), loss (she could no longer be the woman she was only a few minutes ago. That woman had died with Martin, she was Bryant's now. Fully formed in a new image, the image of a woman who wanted to laugh and love again. Who wanted to make love like this).

Her heart hurt, her body ached but it wasn't painful. She thought she would cry, but no tears would come, it was the dissolution of sorrow replaced with joy. She opened her eyes and saw the slope of his shoulder, the curve of his jaw. She wondered if he'd ever felt joy like this before.

In his arms she hadn't been reawakened. She'd been reborn.

Her whole body flooded with electric desire and hunger. She wanted more. More than she'd ever dared dream before.

Bryant gave her a chance for a new life, a new future. As their body moved together in rhythm she tried to catch his eye, but he always looked away. And when he avoided her gaze a third time she began to worry that perhaps this moment didn't mean as much to him as it did to her, until she finally understood.

He didn't want to overwhelm her; he was letting her take the lead. He was letting her feelings, her cravings, and her needs be in the forefront. She thanked him for that. But she also wondered something else.

He'd been considerate of others (sharing how he'd tried to rebuild Esme's confidence; letting Cheryl set the pace in their new relationship), but who had been considerate of him? What was he thinking? Why did he feel near but also far away? Why did he suddenly remind her of a toy that had been abandoned or discarded?

Because in a way he had. She'd loved Martin and he'd loved her. Had anyone ever loved Bryant like that? She knew Esme hadn't. And somehow she sensed that he'd never had that experience. It was something she could give him. She could show him what that felt like.

Cheryl gently touched his cheek and he turned to her sharply. In his gaze she saw surprise, vulnerability and need. Yes, he didn't only want her. He needed her. He needed to know that he was not a replacement for someone else or second best. He quickly looked away and the expression disappeared, but his secret was revealed and she couldn't—wouldn't—ignore it. She wasn't sure she was ready to love him as fully as she'd loved Martin, but she wouldn't betray him as Esme had. There would never be a point that they parted ways without him knowing why.

She turned his face to hers again and kissed him. "Do you like playing with me?"

He nodded, keeping his gaze lowered.

"Are you having fun?"

He nodded again.

"You can look at me now."

He explored her thighs with his hand then slid it to her stomach. "You're like a racetrack."

"A racetrack?"

He nodded. "As a kid I was obsessed with them. I always redesigned the ones that came in the box. They were never what I wanted." His gaze swept over her body. "But you...you're everything I want." He moved his hand up to her chest, over her breast, stopping at a nipple. "Perfect." He covered her breast with his mouth, teasing the nipple with his tongue.

She moaned in pleasure, feeling the warm, wet muscle against her skin. "I hope you weren't doing that to your racetrack."

"No, I think I would have hurt myself."

"I'm not scared."

She felt him pause. "Hmm."

"You can look at me."

His tone deepened. "I am looking at you."

"You're looking at my body."

He bit his lip, his hand moving down her hip. "And enjoying ever inch."

"But you're not looking at my face."

He paused again. "It's better this way."

"Why?"

He kissed her.

And for a moment his persuasive mouth wiped all other thoughts from her mind. It didn't matter if he didn't look at her if he made her feel like this. If his hot mouth could make her feel as if she were burning, cause a liquid heat to build between her thighs.

"Bryant."

"Don't talk," he whispered, joining their bodies together again.

"Bryant?"

He shook his head. "Not yet," he said his voice almost a plea.

She didn't know exactly why he couldn't look at her, but she wouldn't pressure him. This moment was perfect as it was. She playfully bit his ear then said, "I found my new favorite toy."

She felt him smile.

"I like you better than my Excavator."

She felt him grow still.

"I mean it."

He swallowed then shifted his gaze to meet hers. And his searching brown gaze slowly lit with an expression of happiness that made her catch her breath. She'd said what he'd needed to hear.

"Really?"

She nodded then traced a pattern on his chest and said in a coy voice, "Does this mean you're going to stay?"

He laughed and held her close. "You really have to ask me that?"

"I failed to get Esme back."

He tweaked her nose. "Stop acting innocent."

"Innocent?"

"Yes. This was your plan all along."

She released a happy sigh, enjoying his teasing. She closed her eyes and rested against his chest. "Yes, I wanted to have you all to myself. Are you free this Saturday?"

"Hannah's coming for a visit."

Cheryl groaned. "Oh, right. My rival."

He playfully pinched her nose. "I told you it isn't like that. Besides, I'm hoping to convince Ginnie to join us this time."

Cheryl opened her eyes. "That would be good. Take them on a picnic. The weather will be great. I'll pack something for you."

He kissed her on the forehead. "Where's this sweet side coming from?"

"I don't know. You must be good for me."

CHAPTER TWENTY-SIX

She'd never worked so hard for a picnic she wasn't even going to. But she wanted it to work for Ginnie's sake. If Bryant had managed to convince her to come out of her room to spend time with her daughter, Cheryl wanted to do her best to help.

She looked at the loaded basket.

Bryant came into the kitchen. "Are you ready yet?"

"Just about. Give me a few more minutes to wrap these muffins."

He leaned against the island and watched her. "You're free to join us."

"Your rival will kill me."

"Stop calling her that." He lifted the basket lid.

"Leave it alone."

"Can't I even peek?"

"No." She tucked the muffins inside.

Bryant glanced at the door then lowered his voice and said, "Backhoe loader."

178

"What?"

"Can't you tell when a man's talking dirty?"

Cheryl began to laugh recognizing the name of the earth moving equipment. It could be 'dirty' indeed. "Not bad."

"I can do better."

She leaned towards him. "Go ahead."

"Excavator."

"Hmm. That's nice. Keeping going."

"Bulldozer." He glanced down at something then said, "Skid-steel loader, ride-on sweeper."

"Hmm...you know what I like."

He glanced down again. "Trencher."

"Wait, what are you looking at?"

"Nothing."

She came around the island and caught him covering his cell phone.

She snatched it from him and saw the list on the screen. "You're cheating."

Bryant took the phone back and put it away. "Give me a break, I don't know that much about construction."

She laughed. "You could have fooled me. Start talking about an adjustable shovel that can move dirt, backfill and dig trenches and I'm a lost woman."

"Sounds dirty enough to me."

"Or a boning rod."

He slipped a hand around her waist. "You made that up."

Cheryl shook her head. "No, it's real. I'll show you later."

"I could show you one right now."

She wrapped her arms around his neck. "Now you're really getting dirty."

He laughed before he kissed her.

"You lied!"

They quickly broke apart at the angry accusation and turned to see Hannah glaring at them in the doorway.

She took a step forward and pointed at Bryant. "You lied!"

He sighed. "Hannah."

"You said you didn't like her. And you said you weren't friends."

"I didn't lie. At the time...things changed and—"

"They weren't supposed to," she cried before she ran out.

Bryant swore and followed her into the hall. She ran into a closet and closed the door.

He turned the knob, but she held it tight. He knew he could overpower her, but didn't want to. He released his grip and lowered his voice.

"Hannah, what's going on?"

"Why did you lie?"

"I told you, I didn't."

"You told me you didn't like her. You said you felt the same way I did."

"I did, but...now I do like her. I got to know her better. If you gave her a chance you'd like her too."

"I don't want to. I don't like her."

"Why?"

"Why couldn't you have waited?"

He paused. He never seriously imagined that Hannah could have such a large crush on him. Did she really expect him to wait for her to grow up? He softened his tone. "Hannah, come out and let's talk."

"No."

"People's feelings change. But she'll never replace you. You'll always be my friend."

"I don't want to be friends. I want you to be my stepdad."

Bryant briefly closed his eyes. He'd never considered that was her secret hope. She'd wanted him to be with her mother, no wonder she was so upset. "I think being your friend is even better."

"Better?"

"Yes, because no matter what that won't change. If I married your mother and then we divorced I wouldn't be your stepdad anymore, but we can be friends forever and ever and that doesn't depend on anyone else. Do you understand?"

"I wish you loved my mother. She needs..." Her words fell away.

He pressed his palm against the door. "I know."

"She's pretty and smart. You make her happy. I can't," Hannah said sounding miserable.

Bryant tried the doorknob again and this time the door open. He looked down at Hannah's tear stained face. "That's not your fault." He knelt down and held out his arms.

She ran into them and cried.

He lifted her up and patted her back. "It will be okay."

"Can't you change your mind? Please?"

"I don't love your mother. I like her, but that won't change."

He turned to take Hannah with him back into the kitchen hoping to lighten her mood with a sweet muffin, but he stopped when he saw Ginnie standing there.

Pain splashed across her face before she said, "You're not with Esme anymore?"

CHAPTER TWENTY-SEVEN

Cheryl stayed in the kitchen. She hadn't realized the strength of Hannah's feelings and didn't want to interfere.

She put a thermos in the basket, hoping Bryant would be able to calm Hannah down enough so they could enjoy their picnic. The day was perfect for it.

She turned when she heard footsteps and saw Bryant. He looked devastated. She rushed over to him. "What happened? Is she okay now?"

He shook his head; opened his mouth then closed it.

She took his hand and led him to a chair. "Tell me what happened."

Bryant took a deep breath. "I didn't realize how much I was hurting her."

She squeezed his hand then released it. "You can't help a crush."

"I was right. It wasn't a crush."

"Then what is it? Maybe she's lying because she's embarrassed or–?"

"She wants me to marry Ginnie." His hand shook as he covered his eyes. "And I had to break her heart and tell her that would never happen."

"You had to be honest."

His hand fell to his lap. He looked at her. "I should have lied."

"That would have been worse. You can't always sell a dream."

"I hate when I can't make a child smile. I broke her heart."

"No." Cheryl took and held his hand in both of hers and kissed it. "Hannah's heart had been broken before you came along. All you can do is be there for her."

"That's what I thought and then she came."

"Who?"

"Ginnie. She looked at me as if I'd punched her. I didn't realize..." He sighed and pinched the bridge of his nose. "She told me she wasn't feeling well and couldn't make the picnic. Now she's back in her room and Hannah's in the main room sitting on the couch and won't talk. I don't know what to do."

Cheryl nodded, ready to take action. She went to the picnic basket, pulled out a muffin and handed it to him. "You take this to Hannah and keep her company for a few minutes. I'll go talk to Ginnie."

She didn't know what she would say, but she had to say

something. She knew how it felt to not want to face another day, but she didn't have someone else depending on her like Ginnie did. There were certain luxuries a parent didn't have.

She knocked on the door.

"I don't want to talk, Bryant," Ginnie said.

"It's not Bryant. It's me, Cheryl and I think we have to." She opened the door and saw Ginnie in bed with the covers up to her chin, her eyes wide, red from crying. "Do we have to do this?"

"Yes."

"What did Bryant tell you?"

Cheryl sat on the side of the bed. "This isn't about Bryant and we both know that." She looked around the cluttered room at the clothes littering the ground; the plate from another day crusted with dried food. "Holding onto grief doesn't help."

"You must think I'm—"

Cheryl turned to her. "And self-pity is even worse. You're the only mother Hannah has."

"Soon she'll have another one. A better one. Much better than me."

"But she loves you."

"I don't know why."

"Doesn't matter, just be there for her. You don't have to be perfect. And sometimes she'll say things that hurt, but you have to be the bigger person."

Ginnie wiped away a tear and said in a small voice, "I don't think I can. I gave everything to my marriage. I wanted it to work. I wanted Hannah to have the same kind of childhood I did. My parents were happily married for years. I couldn't give her that."

"You wouldn't be the first. And divorce is a loss, but it's not the end. You can try to start again."

"How do you do it? How do you stay here? *Why* do you stay here?"

Cheryl thought for a moment. "If you'd asked me that only a couple months ago I couldn't have given you an honest answer. First the market wasn't good and then I was too busy with work and then I came up with other excuses until I realized I couldn't leave. I didn't want to leave. I feel at home here."

Ginnie nodded. "Home," she said softly. "It didn't really feel like that before, but now it does." She looked at her shyly. "Is it because of Bryant?"

"And Hannah and you," Cheryl said, not willing to give Bryant all the credit, although she knew he was a big part of the reason for the change in the house and within her. "It wouldn't be the same if I were here all by myself."

Ginnie sighed. "I hope I didn't embarrass Bryant. I know that I never really had a chance with him, but it was still nice to think about. I want a different life than this, but I don't even know how to start moving on."

"You can start by coming out of your room more often. Spend more time with Hannah. Have dinner with us sometimes."

"That sounds nice, but I'm not ready for that. I don't think I can be around people in love yet."

Cheryl laughed. "We're hardly in love." She stood to her feet. "And I won't let you use excuses to stay in here. It's a beautiful day, I made a delicious picnic basket and your daughter is waiting for you downstairs. So I'm going to help you get ready and you're going to have a wonderful time with her. I've got a plan."

Ginnie pushed back her sheets. "I used to be a little afraid of you."

Cheryl opened her closet. "You should be."

Ginnie shook her head. "I don't think I can ever be again. I see why Bryant chose you."

Cheryl shrugged feeling embarrassed by her compliment. She pulled out a dress and held it out to her. "I'm sure if the circumstances had been different you would have—"

"I'm not talking about me," Ginnie interrupted, taking the dress. "I'm talking about Esme. I never really thought she was right for him. I'm glad he found you. You understand what's important to him."

Cheryl closed the closet not knowing what else to say. Her feelings were still too new and raw for her to explore further. She noticed a lipstick on the dresser. She lifted it up and turned to Ginnie. She had an urge to tidy up the place, but first she had to make Ginnie look more presentable. "Right now what's important to both of us is helping you make a little girl smile."

CHAPTER TWENTY-EIGHT

*B*ryant waved as Hannah and Ginnie drove away in Ginnie's green Kia. "What did you say to her?" he said amazed as he watched the car merge onto the main road.

Cheryl turned and headed back inside. "Nothing special."

"Nothing special? Ginnie looks like a new woman. That dress... and her face. She's gorgeous."

Cheryl shot him a teasing look. "Are you trying to make me jealous?" She walked into the living room.

He ignored her. "And when she said she was taking Hannah to a special place just the two of them," Bryant shook his head stunned, "I've never seen Hannah so happy."

Cheryl sat on the couch and stared up at him in triumph. "I might have given Ginnie a small pep talk and gotten her tickets to see a laser show in the park and the music is by a popular kid's group. I had my sister pull some strings."

Bryant folded his arms. "I'm jealous."

"You wanted to go too?"

He frowned. "No, I wanted to make Hannah happy like that."

Cheryl shrugged. "I still don't think she likes me."

He sat down beside her, resting his arm around her shoulders. "She should."

Cheryl stared at him. "Why?"

"Because no other woman has a chance with me now. I'm completely yours." His eyes melted into hers. "Thank you."

"For what?" Cheryl asked suddenly feeling breathless.

He drew her close, pressing his lips against hers before he said, "Making a little girl's dream come true."

That evening Hannah came home ready to tell Bryant all that she and her mother had done. Cheryl left them alone in the main room and went to the kitchen with Ginnie.

"I don't know how to thank you," Ginnie said.

"You don't have to." She took the picnic basket from her. "Go and change. You look exhausted."

"I am. But happy too."

Cheryl emptied the basket pleased when she saw all that had been consumed. She caught movement out of the corner of her eye. She looked and saw Hannah standing outside the kitchen entrance. "Hey kid, are you just going to stand there?"

Hannah pushed herself from the doorframe and came forward. She sat on the stool at the island.

"Your mother's getting changed."

"I know. She told me." She fell silent, lowered her gaze, drew a circle on the table with her thumb then said, "I guess I don't hate you anymore."

"Okay."

She looked up surprised. "You still don't care?"

Cheryl shrugged. "It's easier."

"Do you like me?"

"Do you want me to?"

Hannah hesitated then nodded.

"Good because I give my friends chocolate brownies. Would you like one?"

She grinned and nodded again.

Cheryl gave her one she'd been hiding for herself.

Hannah took a bite. "This is the best brownie I've ever had."

"Did someone say brownies?" Bryant said, coming into the room.

"Sorry," Cheryl said. "That was the last one."

His face fell.

"I'll make another batch later."

He eyed Hannah.

"No," Cheryl said with warning. "That's hers."

He walked over to Hannah. "Come on. One little bite."

"Resist him, Hannah."

Hannah giggled.

He sidled up beside her and said in a coaxing tone, "I thought we were friends."

"Leave her alone," Cheryl told him.

He nudged Hannah with his elbow and winked. "Just a little piece."

Cheryl grabbed Bryant's arm and pulled him away. "Hannah run!"

Hannah laughed and raced out of the kitchen.

Bryant sat at the island and rested his forehead on the table. "I can't believe you gave her the last one," he said in a pitiful voice. "And it was a corner piece too."

"I can't believe you were trying to sweet talk it away from her."

He rested his head in his hand. "When it comes to your cooking I have no shame," he said then smiled looking like a mischievous kid and for a wild moment Cheryl thought of what he must have been like as a little boy. Then she wondered what it would be like to have a boy with him or a girl or both. She swallowed, shocked by the strength of her feelings. Could she imagine starting a family with him?

She loved him. That much she could no longer deny. But did he love her? Did she want him to? She chewed her lip. She was scared. She hadn't felt this many emotions in a long time and she found it exhausting. And also exhilarating.

"I have a request," he said.

"We're all out of ingredients for brownies."

He made a face and rested his forehead back on the counter.

She leaned over and whispered in his ear, "However,

I still have a can of whipped cream. Think you could find a use for it?"

He lifted his head, no longer looking like a kid but a very grown man with a sexy grin. "I can think of a few."

~

Sticky and delicious.

Bryant lay in bed with a languid smile.

He'd never look at a can of whipped cream the same way again. Next time he wanted to try honey or chocolate or peanut butter. Perhaps all three. He felt Cheryl shift beside him, her bare thigh brushing his. He remembered licking his way up that thigh and over to her center. He'd surprised her, the tip of his tongue causing her to cry out.

He wanted to keep on surprising her, and tasting her and loving her.

Bryant sighed feeling his good mood dim.

It was too soon. He knew it was too soon to tell her how he felt. But he wanted to be with her. He wanted to always be by her side. He wanted to marry her, but what did he have to offer her? She owned this house. She had her own business. He worked as a toy designer. It had never bothered him before but he wanted to impress her. He saw his failings against Martin's. He was a miniature scale model to the real thing. He sold dreams but how did he sell his dream to her?

He remembered his last phone call with his brother when he told him he was seeing somebody else.

"So when are you going to make it official?" Quentin asked.

He paused surprised by the question. "We just started seeing each other."

"The moment you moved into that house you haven't stopped talking about her. You mentioned how sad she looked, how she hurt Hannah, how angry she is. Then recently it's been all about her cooking and how kind she is to Ginnie. I know you. You've never been like this with any other woman. She's the one for you and you know it."

"I don't think she's ready for that yet."

"But you want to," Quentin pressed him.

He wouldn't deny it. "I'm willing to be patient."

"Or are you scared?"

He nodded. "Yes, that too." He didn't want to lose what he had. He couldn't take her saying no. Esme's rejection had hurt enough, he didn't want to do that again and his feelings for Cheryl flowed even deeper. He didn't want to face that kind of pain.

"Can you stay this way forever?" Quentin asked.

"Sure. As long as I'm her man that's fine."

"You're lying."

"I don't want to think too far ahead."

"At least let her know how you feel."

"When the time is right, I'll—"

"She loves you."

Bryant smiled. "You haven't even met her yet."

"Everything you've told me about her says it."

He wanted to believe that but was afraid to. "Even if she did, which she doesn't, she loved Martin more."

"You're not competing with him. Dad made everything in life like it's a competition. It doesn't have to be that way."

"But it is for me. I'm in another man's place. There's no escaping that. I want to make Cheryl happy the same way he did. That's why I'll be patient."

Bryant sighed as he thought of his brave words only a few days ago. He lightly touched a strand of her hair. How patient would he be? A few years? How long would he put his dreams on hold? And what if he could never convince her to dream with him?

CHAPTER TWENTY-NINE

Azaleas. She hadn't bought azalea bushes in years. After Bryant had destroyed the ones Martin had planted she'd left the driveway empty. But there they were on her coffee table: A large pot of red azaleas.

"I'm sorry," Shawn said, coming into the main room from the direction of the office. "I shouldn't have said what I did the other day."

She sighed. She'd barely seen him over the past couple of days. So much had changed in her life that it felt like months. "And I know I have no right to tell you how to live your life."

"I'm always on your side. If you want me to end it with Esme I will. It's not serious anyway."

"No, you don't have to do that."

He walked up to her and looked at her in a way he never had before. Not as her brother-in-law but as a man. The look made her blush. "I want you to know that you can always trust me," he said, his gaze serious and searching. "I'm here for you no matter what. Even when I'm an idiot."

"I know that."

He held out his arms. "Am I forgiven?"

She hugged him, he felt warm and familiar. "Yes."

"So you don't hate me with the venom of a thousand snakes?"

She laughed and playfully punched him in the shoulder. "Only about a hundred right now."

"What will make you forgive me completely?"

"I'll have to think about it."

He pushed the pot towards her. "I can get a bunch more and help you plant them."

She hesitated. "I'm not sure I want to do the same design as before. I might put them towards the side. Thanks." Someone knocked on the front door. "I'd better get that. Might be a delivery."

Shawn nodded and watched her go then released his breath. He wasn't sure she'd forgive him as easily as she had. But he didn't want to lose her. She was too important to him. Being with Esme wasn't worth the risk.

He turned and saw Bryant, looming like a dark shadow. He jumped and swore. "How long have you been there?"

"Not long."

"Are you trying to scare me?"

"What's that?" He motioned to the pot.

"It's for Cheryl."

"Really?"

He frowned, not liking the other man's tone. "Of

course. They're her favorite. Don't get mad at me because you hadn't thought of it yourself."

He walked into the room. "I'm not mad."

"Good."

"But I don't like you trying to remind her of the past."

"I'm not doing that."

Bryant lowered his gaze and said in a quiet voice, "You have to choose."

"What?"

Bryant pinned him with a look. "You heard me. The past or present. Make a choice."

Shawn shrugged. "I don't know what you're talking about."

"I'm talking about Esme and Cheryl. You can't have it both ways. You can't sleep with Esme and flirt with Cheryl at the same time."

"I wasn't flirting."

Bryant nodded. "That's true. You're in love with her. Did your brother know how you felt about her?"

Shawn grabbed Bryant's collar and shoved him against the wall. "Watch your mouth."

Bryant flashed a sour grin. "I guess the answer is no."

Shawn shoved him against the wall once more then released him and turned. "You're not worth it."

Bryant smoothed down his shirt. "I'll make the choice easy for you. You can have Esme. Cheryl is mine."

Shawn spun around. "You trying to warn me off?"

"It's not a warning."

"Esme dumped you. If you can't hang on to Cheryl, you have no one to blame but yourself. And if I want her, I'll have her."

Bryant shook his head. "No, you won't."

Shawn looked him up and down and sniffed. "My brother could have bench pressed you with his pinky. Stick with your toys and find another woman."

Bryant folded his arms. "How come I get the feeling that you don't like me?"

"You don't even come close to the kind of man my brother was. The only reason Cheryl's with you is loneliness and pity."

"And the only reason she'd turn to you is nostalgia and desperation."

Shawn's face changed from smug to rage. He lunged at him. Bryant managed to duck the first punch but not the second. He staggered back, shook his head and rubbed his jaw. "Not bad." He rolled up his sleeves. "You've got a pretty good punch for a coward."

Shawn lunged for him again, this time Bryant ducked and shouldered him in the stomach. Shawn stumbled back and they ended up on the ground.

"What is going on?" Cheryl asked, rushing into the room. She dropped the delivered package on the floor.

The two men ignored her and continued to fight.

She studied them wondering which one would be easier to grab, but they both seemed like two wild predators—one a panther the other a mountain lion.

"Stop! Cut it out!"

They continued to ignore her until they stumbled into the table knocking over the pot. It crashed to the ground. They stopped and scrambled apart.

Cheryl raced over to the ruined plant and glared up at them. "Are you happy now?"

Shawn dropped to his knees beside her. "I'm sorry. I can get you another one."

"It would have been better if you hadn't ruined the first one." She shot Bryant a look. "Unless you have something against azaleas."

"No," Bryant said, wiping blood from his mouth. "Just the ones that come from him."

Shawn stood. "What's that supposed to mean?"

"Exactly what you think."

Cheryl jumped between them before they could start fighting again. "That's enough. What's wrong with you two?"

Bryant looked at Shawn. "Want me to tell her?"

"Go to hell," he said then stormed out.

CHAPTER THIRTY

Cheryl looked at Bryant stunned. "What happened?"

He shook his head. "Ask him."

"I'm asking you."

He pushed himself from the wall. She blocked him. "Where are you going?"

He glanced at the plant. "To get something to help you clean this up." He moved past her.

Minutes later the soil was cleared up and the azaleas in a new pot, if not a little worse for wear. He set the pot back on the coffee table. "There. Almost like new."

She tilted his chin and looked at his cut lip. "He got you good."

Bryant shrugged. "It's no big deal."

"Let me at least clean the cut. Sit down." She got her First Aid kit, sat down beside him and attended to his bruise. "Shawn isn't usually like that. What did you say to him?"

"Why do you think it was me?"

"Because you still have feelings for Esme."

He sighed and moved her hand from his face. "We weren't fighting about Esme."

"I know you don't want to admit it to me, but it must be hard to see the guy who is with your ex—"

Bryant's tone hardened. "We were not fighting about Esme."

"Then what was it about?"

He started to stand. "You really should ask him."

She pulled him back down. "I'm asking you. Tell me what you were fighting about. What did my azalea nearly risk its life for?"

He rubbed the back of his neck then said softly, "You."

"Me?"

He nodded. "We were fighting about you."

"What is there to fight about?"

He sent her a pointed look.

She smiled amused. "You don't have to worry about Shawn. We're family. Like brother and sister."

"I'm not sure he sees it that way."

"He's seeing Esme now."

Bryant frowned. "Don't underestimate him."

"I'm sure it was all a misunderstanding."

"Maybe," he said but he didn't sound convinced.

"Come on," she said, feigning a light tone to ease the tension in the room. "Admit it. You hate azaleas. Something happened in your childhood and you have some secret vendetta against them."

His expression didn't change.

"That was a joke." She frowned. "Why are you staring at me like that?"

"You don't understand me yet."

Cheryl's pulse quickened. Damn, she'd said something wrong. What had she said wrong? "What do you mean?"

He lowered his gaze and took her hand in his. "I'm with you now."

"I know that."

He caught and held her gaze. "Then why would you think I was fighting about Esme?"

Cheryl blinked quickly, searching her mind for the right response. "I don't know...it just looked that way."

Bryant closed his eyes and pressed a fist against his forehead. "Tell me what I'm doing wrong."

"You're not doing anything wrong," she said surprised.

He pounded his thigh, his jaw clenched. "Then why..." He paused, took a deep breath then tried again. "Esme was shocked that I cared about her and now you're acting the same."

"It's not that. It's not you. It's just...it's her. She's amazing."

"So are you."

"I don't look like her."

Bryant stared at her confused. "You don't have to."

Cheryl looked away feeling suddenly shy and ridiculous. He was right. He was with her. He'd shown how much he liked her, what more did she need? He didn't need her to list all her failings. It was clear that she wasn't anything like Esme in terms of looks, background or profession. "I'm sorry."

He squeezed her hand. "You don't have to be sorry. Just tell me what I have to do to let you know how I feel." He bit his lip. "I know I'm not like Martin—"

"You don't have to be," she said quickly. "I don't want you to be. I like you just the way you are."

He nodded. "And I feel the same."

She narrowed her eyes. "You promise that fight wasn't about Esme?"

"Yes."

"So Shawn thinks you still want her back?"

Bryant sent her a long look. "I told you we were fighting about you, not Esme."

"I'll talk to him. He's probably being protective."

"No, leave him alone for now. He needs space and he has to come to a decision. It won't be easy."

CHAPTER THIRTY-ONE

That bastard saw right through him. Cheryl had never seen him as a man. When he'd first met her he'd had feelings, but she was his brother's girlfriend. Then when Martin passed he had a faint hope that, with time perhaps, she'd turn to him for comfort and return his feelings. And maybe she would have if Hill hadn't entered the picture. He and Cheryl were close. He was the only person she would confide in and talk to.

But he'd never been able to make her come out of her shell the way Bryant had. Even though it had started as a farce she'd never dress up and go to a function with him. No matter how much he dreamed of it. That night, when he saw her in the red dress, she'd taken his breath away. Now she smiled and laughed just like she used to. It hurt that he hadn't been the cause or the reason.

You have to choose.

He didn't want to. He liked having both Esme and Cheryl in his life. He had hope that Cheryl seeing him with another woman would force her to see how desirable he was; that he could be the man for her; to see him in a new light, but that hadn't happened. At least not yet, but it could. An innocent flirtation could turn into more.

You have to choose.

And what if he didn't? What would Hill do? Was he afraid he didn't have her completely? But he didn't want to lose Cheryl either by revealing his feelings. He hated to admit that Hill was right and the worst part was the choice had already been made for him.

"Are you thinking about her?"

Shawn turned to Esme who lay in bed beside him. He looked around her expansive bedroom with its antique bed and handmade Moroccan rug. He could lie. Part of him wanted to and a part knew there was no reason to. "Are you thinking about him?"

She sighed and he knew the answer. "We should stop seeing each other. We know this is going nowhere."

She was right, he knew this moment would come but part of him wanted to deny it. Pretend they weren't both hurting somehow. That they weren't using each other. It was working, right? Why fix it. But it wouldn't get any better than this. Great sex and silence afterwards. Soon the silence would stretch out to nothing.

He knew he'd been on borrowed time. She was like a lottery win. A one in a million chance for a guy like him. He'd never expected to hang on to the lucky ticket for long but he wanted to try.

"We could go out some time," he said.

She trailed a finger down his chest. "What's the point? I don't like chit chat."

"I like you."

A slow, secretive smile touched her lips. "You don't even know me."

"I like what I know so far."

"And that's all you'll get to know."

"Why did you break the engagement off with Hill?"

She turned away and sat up, giving him an enviable view of her naked back. "Cheryl can have him."

"That's not what I asked you."

"Why didn't you tell Cheryl how you feel?"

He nodded. They weren't willing to open up to each other. They had their secrets. He'd keep his and she'd keep hers. He sat up and grabbed his pants. "It's been fun."

"Right," she said and he knew it was another way of saying goodbye.

CHAPTER THIRTY-TWO

*E*sme changed into her nightgown and sighed. She hadn't really wanted to end it with Shawn, even though she knew it would end eventually, but she couldn't keep this charade up for long. First she never liked to spend time with a man who was thinking about another woman (that was annoying) and second her mother was on to her. Her mother's scolding the other day still irked her.

"It's time you stop this nonsense," her mother said, meeting her in the foyer as Esme walked through the door. She'd returned from work and just wanted to relax, but from the expression on her mother's face those hopes were dashed.

She put her keys in the bowl in the hall. "What nonsense?"

"A contractor? Really?"

"Don't be a snob."

"When are you getting back with Bryant?"

She headed to the stairs. "I'm not."

"And what will you do when your father hands over the company to him?"

She sharply turned to her. "What do you mean?"

"Don't look at me like that. Do you think I wasn't thinking about your future when you two started dating? Bryant came into this company and nearly single-handedly saved it. Something you hadn't managed to do."

Her face heated. It was a sore point her mother continued to like pointing out. She'd missed certain signs and opportunities with the toy that had hit the market and been a critical and commercial flop. If Bryant hadn't come on board they may have lost the business. She was used to being on top—in class, in life, in business. It had hurt her pride to fail so spectacularly in the real world. But she'd grown since then and now felt comfortable that she could run the business and make her father proud. "I've learned a lot from Bryant and Dad knows that. He wouldn't—"

"He would and he will. He wants a legacy. He wants this business to last. He doesn't care who does it." She softened her voice. "Marriage isn't all romance and chocolates. Bryant is a good man and an asset. Don't let him go."

At that moment she came to a decision. She wouldn't let him go.

Unfortunately, one thing stood in her way.

Cheryl.

Esme frowned and grabbed some lotion to lather her skin. She started with her legs. How could Shawn even have feelings for her? She didn't like the fact that he was using her to get over Cheryl, although she'd been doing the same to him with Bryant. But she didn't have the same feelings for Bryant as Shawn did for Cheryl.

She wanted Bryant back not because she wanted him, but because it would make her mother happy and help her career. But she also had another reason.

She didn't want Cheryl to have him. It was bad enough she had Shawn longing for her, she didn't need to have Bryant too.

Esme lathered her arms, pensive. She just needed to find a way to get him back. There was still time and she knew a lot more about Bryant than she let on.

She called Shawn.

"You changed your mind?" he asked.

She got right to the point. "Do you want Bryant out of the picture?"

He hesitated. "What do you have in mind?"

"A little blackmail. There's something Cheryl should know about him."

She hadn't come into his office in weeks. The moment Esme knocked on the door and entered, Bryant went on alert. She was up to something, from the composed expression on her face, which reminded him too much of her mother, it was something big. Bryant sat back and watched her take a seat. "What's up?"

Esme crossed her legs. "So does she know?"

"Does who know what?"

"Does Cheryl know the state of your health?"

Bryant took a deep breath, tempering down the shot of panic that coursed through his body. He wouldn't worry. She wanted to provoke him, he couldn't let that happen. "What do you want?"

"Shawn told me that she lost her husband. I think she should know about—"

"I'm healthy now."

"You weren't always this—"

"This doesn't concern you."

"Yes, it does," she said in a tight voice. "I made a mistake. I admit it. Just like I did years ago with this company and you helped me get out of it. I'm asking for that chance again. Please. I want another chance."

Bryant sighed and shook his head. "Esme—"

"I know you used her to get back at me. That's your style not hers. From what Shawn has told me, she's a really good woman."

He rested his chin in his hand, looking bored. "You don't sound like you believe that."

"I don't really like her, but from what he said—"

"So you think you know everything about Cheryl because of what he said?"

"He's known her longer than you have. I'm just warning you—"

His expression grew hard, his tone cold. "Warning me?" He leaned forward and clasped his hands together on the desk. "Why didn't you warn me two years ago that you were never in love with me, never would be. It would have been nice if you'd warned me that I was only a nice part of your plan. I wouldn't have gotten my hopes up."

Esme stared at him stunned. "Wasn't I part of your

plan too? You had me fit just where you liked me and I was never let out of that spot."

"I didn't hear any complaints."

"There's no point bringing up the past. My mother—"

Bryant shook his head almost pained. "Please don't tell me that's the reason you came to me. Oh, I get it. Shawn isn't good enough. He doesn't meet your mom's standards. Too late, I'm with Cheryl now."

"I told him."

He stared at her. "You what?"

"I told him about your diagnosis. If you don't break it off with Cheryl, he'll tell her."

Panic surged through him again. *I can't lose Cheryl. Not because of this. Please don't do this to me.* He gripped his hands tighter. He couldn't show weakness. Esme had hurt him once before, he wouldn't let that happen again. She couldn't know how much power she had. "I don't care. She'll understand."

She folded her arms with a smirk. "You don't sound confident."

"I am."

"Then why didn't you tell her before?"

He looked away, he knew the reason but wouldn't tell her. He'd hoped Cheryl would never have to know. Or at least keep his past from her for several more months. He needed time for her to trust him and care about him to risk loving him as he was. Her knowing would ruin everything.

Esme leaned forward and softened her tone. "I'm doing this for your own good."

He met her gaze, wary. "Why don't I believe that?"

"Our engagement can impact both our careers."

"One more than the other I bet."

"Bryant."

He placed his palms flat on the table, pleased they were still and gave nothing away. Calm and controlled that was the only way he'd get through this. "You don't know me very well."

Esme rolled her eyes. "Of course I do. I—"

"I asked you to marry me because I loved you. I really thought you loved me too. It wasn't for a promotion, for your parents or any other reason. There was no plan. Just you and me together forever. That was it. That was my dream."

"That doesn't have to change. I admit I made a mistake. I didn't realize how much...I want another chance. We don't have to throw away two years. I know everything about you. There's nothing you had to hide from me. I care about you. When I said yes to your proposal I meant it."

"Then you changed."

"I told you I made a mistake. Can't you forgive me?"

"Yes. I forgive you."

She released a breath in relief. "Then you understand what I'm saying."

"I do," he said simply. "You're scared your father will give me the business."

She stared at him alarmed. "That's not—"

"Your mother has hinted at it too."

"You know this business means everything to me,"

Esme said in a rush. "And I feel the same about you too, but that's not why I'm here. I wanted—"

"To blackmail me so you can get what you want."

She shook her head, looking a little miserable. "It's not like that. It's...it's not something you should hide from her and I'm letting you know I accept you as—"

Bryant sighed, sad. "You win."

"What do you mean?"

He stood. "I'm going to help you make your dreams come true."

CHAPTER THIRTY-THREE

Something was terribly wrong.

Cheryl watched Bryant as he picked at his dinner. He'd never done that before. Martin had the same look when he got sick...

"Oh, God. What happened?"

He looked up at her. "What?"

"You've got bad news to tell me. I can see it."

He hesitated.

She gripped her hands together. "What is it?"

He set his fork down.

She covered her mouth. "Is it bad? Are you...sick?"

He swore. "No, not anymore. It's nothing that you need to be worried about."

"Tell me."

He bit his lip. "I should have told you this sooner, but...I'm... This won't change—"

"Bryant, you're scaring me. What do you have?"

"I'm in remission."

She stared at him, a slow horror crossing her face. "Remission? You had cancer?"

"Yes, but—"

"How long has it been?" she said her voice hard.

"Nearly four years."

Her voice shook. "Why didn't you tell me this before?"

"Cheryl, please."

"You should have told me this before I fell—" She bit her lip. "You said you didn't want to hurt me and yet you kept this from me."

"Not on purpose. I didn't think about it. What's happened between us surprised me too. I never thought... I never expected us to... There's nothing to worry about. I'm better now."

"There's always something to worry about when it comes to cancer. You—"

"The chances are good that I'll live a long life."

Her voice grew soft. "But you can't promise me that it won't return."

"No," Bryant said with a note of regret, his eyes pleading. "I can't promise you that. But I can promise you—"

Cheryl held up her hands. "Stop. I don't want to hear about promises or dreams or the future or anything." She stood and started to clear the dishes. "I need time to think about this. What this means for us."

"I'm still the same man," his voice cracked in misery. "I—" He stopped, afraid that what he wanted to share would hurt her more. He wanted to tell her how much he fought to live, but he knew that was unfair to Martin.

Hadn't Martin fought just as much? Hadn't he wanted to live? He'd gotten lucky, there was nothing special about him. No reason why he was sitting there with her and Martin wasn't.

"I'm not sure I can do this again," Cheryl said with tears. "I'm sorry." She fled the room.

Bryant sat in the empty kitchen wondering if a heart could withstand breaking twice. He pulled out his cell phone and texted Esme. *I told her.*

What did she say?

Anguish gripped him so tight it felt like a physical pain. He fought against his loneliness and despair as he sent back a reply that he wished to be true but knew was a lie. *She accepts me. She loves me anyway. She wants to stay with me.*

He stared at his screen waiting for a reply he knew wouldn't come. He hadn't told Esme what she wanted to hear. He waited a few more seconds then flipped his cell phone faced down and sat back, his gaze looking around the empty kitchen once again. Why did he always end up alone?

Because you're a loser.

He lived in another man's house, loved another man's wife, was building the legacy of another man's business. When would he have something to claim as his own? Did he deserve it? Could he ever face Cheryl again knowing she would probably wish that Martin was alive and he was dead?

His cell phone alerted him to another text. He looked at the message and saw it was from Marlon asking to meet him first thing tomorrow.

He was going to be alone tonight and had a sneaking suspicion he'd be out of a job tomorrow.

From the expression on Marlon's face the following morning at the office, Bryant knew he'd guessed right.

"Esme's threatening to quit," Marlon said in a grim tone. "She's not sure she can work in the same company as you."

Bryant sat in front of him and nodded. "I see."

"The thing is…you're a great asset."

"You don't have to say more. If the choice is between me and her, she wins hands down. She's family. The problem is she doesn't know that. She thinks the exact opposite."

Marlon frowned. "Why would she think that?"

"You'd have to ask her. And you can let her know that she doesn't have to leave. I'll go instead."

Marlon sighed with regret. "It's not easy getting a job in our industry." He clasped his hands together. "You and Esme are great together. You've only been apart a couple of months. My wife and I have had little spats that have lasted much longer. You can build your life here with us."

"I'm in love with someone else."

Marlon paused then nodded resigned. "She must be quite a woman if you're willing to give this up."

"She is."

"She might not be so understanding with a man who's not employed."

"Maybe."

Marlon held out his hand. "I'll miss you. And appreciate all you've done for us."

It was a somber mood as Bryant packed up his things.

Marie wiped her eyes and he gave her a hug and said, "Don't cry."

He stepped into the elevator, wondering where his life would lead him next. A hand stopped the elevator doors from closing. "You can't quit," Esme said.

"It's either you or me."

"This company needs you."

"No, it doesn't. Not anymore. It has you."

"But—"

"You're smart, innovative. You made a mistake before but that's what happens when you're learning. The point is your father trusts you. Your mother was wrong. He wants to leave the business to you. You don't have to marry anyone or do anything to change that. Live your life on your terms."

"I'm really sorry about this."

"It's okay. It's time for me to move on anyway."

"But you really liked it here. Is there any way I can convince you to stay on? I could get you a promotion?"

"I have a few ideas I'd like to try on my own."

Esme narrowed her eyes, suspicious. "You're going to become a competitor, aren't you?"

"No," Bryant said with a slight grin. "My specialty will be different. But don't be surprised to see me at trade shows."

She hesitated. "I should have told you this before. My life has always run according to a certain plan, but I'm not sure I want it. I don't want kids and I'm not sure I even want to get married, but I do want to run Scott Designs with my father and take it as far as it can go."

Bryant nodded. "I know. I realized that was your

dream. One day you need to tell your mother. She won't like it, but it's your life not hers."

Esme's eyes filled with tears. "Thanks."

"For what?"

"Loving me. You were always standing up for me, listening to my ideas, siding with me at meetings, teaching me about the business and caring about me in so many different ways. I'm sorry I didn't see how much until too late."

Bryant shook his head. "I loved you, but not in the way you needed me to. The next man won't make that mistake. Just promise me one thing."

"What?"

"When he tells you he loves you, believe him."

CHAPTER THIRTY-FOUR

*H*e was now out of a job.

Bryant walked up to his room wondering if he'd soon be out of a place to stay. He set his box on the ground then lay on his bed.

Cheryl had wanted to keep him as a tenant so he had that in his favor. But he wasn't sure he could stay with how he felt about her.

He sat up when he heard a knock on the door. Was Cheryl coming to him after all? He smoothed down his shirt and stood, eager. "Come in."

Shawn entered.

His heart fell, he sat back on his bed. "I already told Cheryl about my health."

"I know Esme told me. But I know what you told her was a lie because I saw Cheryl this morning and she didn't look like things were alright between you." He rested his hands on his hips. "I know I'm the last person you want to see right now, but hear me out. You're right. I am a coward. I know I'm not the right guy for her because as much as I love her, she intimidates me. I couldn't have changed her the way you did. I know I can't make her happy the way you can. Cheryl's meeting with a client in an hour, but she'd alone right now. I think you should talk to her."

Bryant shook his head. "She doesn't want to see me."

"Have you told her that you love her?"

"It won't make a difference."

Shawn sniffed. "Who's being the coward now?"

Bryant gripped his hand into a fist. A challenge. He didn't want to be a loser or a coward. He would put everything on the line. He wouldn't hold his feelings back. He wouldn't live afraid. He ran to her office door and walked in when she answered. He held up his hand when she opened her mouth. "Let me speak, first. I know you wish Martin was here instead of me. I can't change that. I can't build you a house. I can't tell the difference between a boning rod and a lightning rod. I've never bench pressed anything in my life, but I can tell you this. I want to be with you for the rest of my life. I can't make any promises, but I can make you a vow. And that is that I will always love you. I know Martin—"

"Enough," Cheryl said. She took a deep breath and shook her head. "I don't need you to be Martin." She put a piece of paper on the desk. "What do you think of this?"

Bryant didn't move, his heart racing.

"Go on," she urged him. "Look at it."

He looked down and saw a blueprint of a room. He didn't understand. Was she telling him to leave? That she'd find him another place to live? Was he being rejected again? "What is it?"

Cheryl came from around her desk and stood next to him. "It's something I want to build for you. I've already chosen an unused room that will be perfect. It's a studio."

"Studio?"

"A toy designer needs a studio, right?" She pointed to a corner section of the blueprint. "This is where your computer would be with enough space for your Wacom and here would be a table for you to test things out."

Bryant stared at her, his lingering fear turning to joy. She wasn't rejecting him. "You'd build this for me?"

It was the expression of joy on his face that nearly undid her. The moment Bryant had come into the office she'd wanted to run into his arms and tell him that she was sorry. Sorry for not being strong enough to face her fears. But she was stronger now. That moment in the kitchen when he'd told her about his health, she thought she saw Death again. That Bryant would always represent that to her. She'd stayed in her room, hiding like Ginnie used to.

But then she remembered why Bryant liked to make toys. Because he liked to play. And playing made her think of kids and laughter and being alive.

And being alive—truly alive—wasn't about anger, fear or hating death. She wouldn't let the past steal any more time from her.

She looked at Bryant now loving every inch of him and feigned a nonchalance that was quickly slipping away, but she had to keep herself together and tell him what she felt before she completely fell apart. "I love building things." She folded her arms, her voice a little unsteady. "I admit I was afraid last night. I didn't want to face the possibility of losing you. But then I realized that all this time I've been living my life afraid and I don't want to do that anymore. Martin wanted me to look towards the future and building things gives me a chance to do that. "

Bryant paused, studying her intently. "Would you consider building a family too?"

"Only with the man I love." Cheryl shot him a teasing grin. "Are you offering to help me?"

In one forward motion, she was in his arms, exactly where she wanted to be. "Absolutely," he said.

"Then the answer is yes," she said, with tears in her eyes and bliss in her heart, then she sealed her vow with a kiss.

ABOUT THE AUTHOR

Dara Girard, an award-winning, national bestselling author of more than forty novels, from romance to suspense, loves telling stories.

Born in the US to immigrant parents, Dara enjoys pulling from her Jamaican, British, Nigerian heritage and exposure to various cultures to bring what reviewers and fans call "vivid emotional stories" to life. She is best known for her popular Henson Series, the mysterious Clifton Sisters, and the fun Black Stockings Society.

You can write her at:
contactdara@daragirard.com
or
P.O. Box 10345
Silver Spring, MD 20914
If you'd like to receive a reply, please send a self-addressed stamped envelope.

Visit her website to sign up for her newsletter and get sneak peeks, monthly updates on new releases, and special offers.

For more information visit
www.daragirard.com